PUFFIN BOOKS

THE GENIUS AND OTHER IRISH STORIES

I can see now, of course, that he didn't really like me ... He had never expected to be the father of a genius and it filled him with forebodings. He looked round him at all his contemporaries who had normal, bloodthirsty, illiterate children, and shuddered at the thought that I would never be good for anything but being a genius.

Frank O'Connor's classic story of childhood is the title story in this dramatic and rich collection of Irish stories, centred specifically on young people's lives and experiences. Some of the best Irish writing is here, including work by Brendan Behan, Edna O'Brien, Joan Lingard, Liam O'Flaherty and Brian Friel. The recurrent and universal themes of family and relationships, wisdom and innocence and, above all, courage, are explored with insight, sympathy and humour.

This is a particularly rewarding collection for all young people.

The Genius
and other Irish Stories

CHOSEN BY GORDON JARVIE
ILLUSTRATED BY CIARAN HUGHES

PUFFIN BOOKS

To Frances

PUFFIN BOOKS

Published by the Penguin Group
27 Wrights Lane, London W8 5TZ, England
Viking Penguin Inc., 40 West 23rd Street, New York, New York 10010, USA
Penguin Books Australia Ltd, Ringwood, Victoria, Australia
Penguin Books Canada Ltd, 2801 John Street, Markham, Ontario, Canada L3R 1B4
Penguin Books (NZ) Ltd, 182–190 Wairau Road, Auckland 10, New Zealand

Penguin Books Ltd, Registered Offices: Harmondsworth, Middlesex, England

First published 1988
10 9 8 7 6 5 4 3 2 1

This selection copyright © Gordon Jarvie, 1988
Illustrations copyright © Ciaran Hughes, 1988
The acknowledgements on pages 161–2 constitute an extension of this copyright page
All rights reserved

Made and printed in Great Britain by
Richard Clay Ltd, Bungay, Suffolk
Filmset in Monophoto Baskerville

Contents

Introduction

Once upon a time, a young man set out from his native Scotland to learn about the great wide world. First of all, he travelled over the sea to Ireland where he studied many of the world's writers and thinkers. Irish scholars of the day helped him find some of the knowledge and wisdom which he sought. Not surprisingly, the young man became very interested in Irish writing. His interest was sharpened by not merely reading but meeting and listening to lectures by Frank O'Connor; by catching frequent sight of Brendan Behan at the pub; and by watching Micheal MacLiammoir perform with panache his famous one-man show at the Gate Theatre in Dublin.

Have you guessed? Of course you have – the young man in question was me. One day I may make time to complete his story, but not here. For the present I will simply recall my excitement at 'discovering' modern Irish literature during my time as a student in Ireland in the early 1960s. The short story is a very powerful strand in Irish literature, and it was in the sixties that I read some of the 'classics' of the short story – work by Liam O'Flaherty, Sean O'Faolain and Walter Macken in addition to the writers named above. Revisiting Irish writing much more recently, I was pleased to find a wide range of interesting contemporary authors, and I include several in this collection: Clare Boylan, Sam McBratney and Bernard MacLaverty.

It is a particular pleasure to draw your attention to a story specially written for this anthology by Joan Lingard, and published here for the first time. Altogether about a third of the stories in this collection were written specifically for younger readers. The remaining two-thirds are really stories for all age-groups to enjoy.

With one or two exceptions, the emphasis in this anthology is on 'realistic' stories, since there is a vast amount of published material for younger readers in the field of Irish myths, legends and folklore. On the other hand, there are very few collections of realistic material for younger readers: I am aware of only two, and one is a school textbook for an older readership with examinations in mind. I hope the present volume will go a little way to make good this deficiency.

I should like this collection to encourage non-Irish readers unfamiliar with Irish writing to explore these authors from a culture different from their own. Here are some wonderful stories which deserve to be universally known. There are, moreover, two advantages to studying another culture: first, we improve our understanding and appreciation of that culture, and secondly, we are helped to a better understanding of our own culture. Finally, I hope Irish readers will enjoy the book enough to forgive the presumption of a mere adoptive Irishman in offering this personal collection.

G.J.
1988

The Lion

WALTER MACKEN

Tim stood patiently at the edge of the small crowd and waited for the appearance of the man he called Putrid in his mind.

He was a young boy. His thin hands were clasped behind his back. This was the third day he had come to watch the feeding of the animals of the circus. Tim hadn't been inside to see the circus. He could never raise the price of it, even the matinée, but the feeding of the animals was for free. Anybody could come and watch. It was a small menagerie. Just a lioness and a tiger and a few monkeys, and Samson.

Samson was the lion. It was near his cage Tim always stood. It wasn't a big cage. It barely fitted the body of the lion. Tim felt his own limbs cramped when he looked at the cage.

Samson wasn't like a lion you would see in books or a picture. His mane was not bushy. It was nearly all worn away. There was only a bit of it left around his head, up near his ears. He didn't roar either. Even when he was provoked he would only loose off a sort of half-hearted growl. You know the sort of small bush that a lion has near the end of his tail. Samson didn't have that either. It was worn away. His tail was mottled, sort of mean-looking. You could see his ribs too. He wasn't a fat lion. Tim was very fond of Samson. He preferred him to the others; to the pacing tiger with the fearful eyes and to the yawning lioness. He even preferred him to the monkeys, although the monkeys were good fun.

The other children had run up to the far side of the field. There was Putrid coming out with the bucket. It was a bucket of meat. Raw meat. The sides of the bucket were stained with old blood and fresh blood. Tim felt the wave of dislike coming over him again at the sight of the man with the bucket.

He was a small man, very black-haired, always seeming to want a shave. He was carrying a pole in his hand with a steel prod on the end of it. Tim felt the muscles of his stomach tightening at the sight of him. Always the same. Opening the slot in the cage of the tiger and the lioness and poking in the meat to them. He talked to those nicely enough always. They grabbed the meat and held it between their claws and squatted at the eating of it. Then he turned his face towards the cage of Samson and went into his act.

Before he could start the act, Tim turned to Samson, and he said to him: 'Don't mind him, Samson. Don't mind him. He is very ignorant.' Samson may have heard him. He turned his head towards him and blinked his great eyes, and then went back to his dreaming. Almost against his will Tim turned his eyes to watch Putrid.

There he was several yards away, crouching like an ape, the bucket in one hand, the pole in the other. The kids were around about him, laughing at his antics.

'Here's the fiercest one of them all, min',' he was saying,

pointing Samson with his nose, like a dog. 'Fresh outa the jungles of Africa. Looka the red in his eyes. Watch the stretch of the claws. Only to be approached with great caution. Careful with him now. He can stretch a limb five foot through the bars to get at ye.'

He circled around as if he was stalking. Tim watched him in disgust. Samson never got anything from him but the bare leavings of the others. The kids were delighted with Putrid. They started to imitate him, crouching and stalking and laughing. Suddenly Putrid darted towards the cage, inserted the prod and stuck it in Samson's side. The lion moved, almost grunting. He couldn't move far. He didn't growl. He didn't roar. Tim would have given anything to hear him roaring with anger. He didn't.

'See that,' says Putrid. 'Hear the roaring of him. Waken the dead he would. Oh, a fierce animal, kids. But, you don't have to be afraid of him. Watch this.' He left down the bucket and the pole and he ran crouching behind the cage and caught hold of Samson's tail. He pulled it as hard as he could, so that the body of the lion was pulled back to the end bars.

'See that,' he was shouting. 'The only fierce animal in captivity to be held be the tail. He'll go mad, so he will. Watch him tear the cage to pieces.'

Tim's finger-nails were biting into his palms. Samson rose almost wearily, straightening himself, crouching because he could not stand upright in the cage, pulling against the pull on his tail, almost staggering on his pads as Putrid suddenly released him. The lion's head hit the bars on the other side. He didn't object.

Because he's old, I suppose, Tim thought. He wouldn't have done that to him when he was young. He conjured up a picture of Samson meeting Putrid in a jungle clearing. Samson wouldn't be unkind then, Tim bet. He would just tear Putrid to pieces. Tim savoured that.

Putrid rubbing his hands.

'Nothin' to it, min',' he was saying. 'I've pulled lions be the

5

tail in every continent in the world. But this one is real fierce when he's feedin'. Oh, real fierce when he's feedin'.'

He didn't open the slot. He pulled the bar and opened the whole door of the cage. Tim wished that Samson would spring out on top of him. He didn't. Putrid hit him on the head with the prod. You could hear the sound of it. Samson just blinked his eyes and pulled back.

'No play in him at all today,' said Putrid. 'Here, Fanny, have your chips.' He up-ended the bucket and flung the contents of it straight into the lion's face. The lion must have looked funny with the things on his face. The bystanders were dying laughing. The scraps fell off his face then on to the floor of the cage.

Putrid banged the door and locked it.

'Bah,' he said. 'No play for him at all today. What a lion. Come on, we'll get to the monkeys.'

They followed him. One of them, before going, tentatively took a pull at the lion's tail which was still hanging through the bars. He let it go quickly and ran after them shouting. 'Hey, fellas, I did it. I pulled his tail.'

Putrid patted him on the head.

'Man,' he said, 'you'll be a lion-tamer yet, so you will.'

They laughed.

Tim was looking at Samson.

'Maybe he doesn't mean it,' he was saying to him. 'But don't mind him. He has to die sometime and then he won't be after you.'

He felt tears in his eyes. Because I'm young, he thought. Like you would cry about a drowning kitten.

Samson started to clean his face. It took him some time. Then he sniffed at the food between his paws. It didn't interest him. He lifted his head and looked away at the sky.

At this moment Tim got the thought that maybe Samson was sick. He knew they didn't use him in the circus. Just the lioness and the tiger. They just carted him around to be a father, they said. And suddenly in his mind's eye he saw the wood outside the town. You came down a hill to it and climbed another hill out of it, and in the hollow there was a clear stream that babbled over stones, and the wood was wide and dappled with sunlight. A place like that Samson would be at home, with the birds and the trees and the bracken, and he would get well and growl and roar and nobody would disturb him, and Putrid couldn't torture him.

On this thought, Tim reached up (he had to stretch a lot) and he pulled back the steel bolt and he opened the door of the cage.

'Come on, Samson,' he said, 'I will take you to a place that you will like. It won't be like the jungle. But it'll be nearly as good. Come on! Please come on before anybody comes.'

Samson didn't want to come.

Tim pulled himself up on to the floor of the cage until he was hanging on his chest. He stretched an arm until his hand could take hold of the remaining mane and he tugged at it gently.

'Come on, Samson,' he said. 'Come on.'

Samson resisted, but then he started to go with the pull of the boy's hand. Tim got his feet on the ground. He still kept his grip on the old lion's mane. And then Samson crouched and sprang to the earth. He stood there for a while, feeling the unaccustomed ground under his pads. Then he dutifully followed the pull of the small hand on his mane and walked beside him, past the caravans, out the gate and into the street of the town.

They walked calmly down the middle of it.

If you can ripple a pond with a pebble you can entirely upset it by throwing a large boulder into it. The pond will explode. It was like that now with the town as the first person looked at the boy and the lion.

This was a fat woman with a shopping basket. She looked and she looked again, and then she dropped her basket and opened her mouth very widely and screamed and turned and ran screaming.

7

Everybody claimed afterwards that it was this woman who led to the unnatural panic with her screaming. Only for her, they said, nobody would have paid the least attention to the boy and the loose lion. Perhaps, but if you are walking up a street and you see a lion walking towards you, I doubt if you will stop to ask any questions. Your skin will crawl, your mouth will dry, the hair will rise on the back of your neck and you will seek safety in flight. Everybody did now. The street, thronged with people, cleared as if a plague had swept through it. People ran into the first open shop door, fighting to get in and to bang the doors behind them, and peer out through the glass. Screaming women and shouting men, all panic-stricken. They ran into cars and closed the doors of them and shot up the windows of them, and peered palely through them.

Tim walked solemnly on, talking to Samson, almost unconscious of the confusion and upset he was leaving behind him. He turned from the busy shopping and market street into the wide Square. This was roomier and people had more time to find safety and to reflect.

Tim paused at the top of the Square and became aware of all the disturbance he was causing and also became aware of the line of police gradually and very cautiously closing in on him. His hand tightened on Samson, and he stopped, and Samson stopped and looked at the circle of men approaching him. He raised a lip and snarled, and the advancing line came to a dead stop, all except the Inspector, a tall man with blue eyes, who came close to the boy and the lion with nothing under his arm except a light cane. He had sense. He had called the circus people. Out of the corner of his eye he saw them approaching now, out of the street into the Square, loaded with ropes and bars and hauling a cage on wheels which they lifted down from a van.

'Take it easy, boy,' said the Inspector. 'Don't get excited. Nothing will happen. Don't excite him.'

Tim's mouth was dry. He suddenly realized that his hopes were at an end. He hadn't thought of the town and the police.

If he could have gone a back way, nobody might have noticed. Now, he thought sadly, Samson would never see the wood.

The Inspector was surprised as he closed on him. The boy had no fear, and as he looked closely at the lion, he saw there was no need for anybody to fear. All the same, who knew? The lion looked old and thin and helpless, but one slash at the boy was all that was needed.

The men were closing from behind, cautiously, the ropes held in loops.

'Leave the lion and come here to me,' said the Inspector.

Tim shook his head.

'No, no,' he said, his small hand tightening on the lion.

'You'll have to leave him go,' said the Inspector. 'The men are behind you. They are going to throw ropes over him. You'll have to come to me.'

'Don't let Putrid touch him,' said Tim.

The Inspector didn't know what he was talking about.

'All right,' he said.

'Goodbye, Samson,' said Tim then, pressing his hand deeply into the lion's neck. He didn't look at him any more. He bent his head and walked to the Inspector. The Inspector heaved a sigh and caught his hand. He watched for a short time as the ropes landed, and the lion was secured. Like a pent-up breath relieved, there was laughter and calling and shouting. He noticed the small, black, dirty little fellow cavorting around the lion as they put him into the cage. He went docilely, peacefully. But this chap was acting the mickey for the surrounding people. And they were laughing at his antics.

'All right,' said the Inspector, 'let's go down and get off the streets and see what this is all about.'

Tim soon found himself alone in a small room with just a desk and a bright fire, and the Inspector who didn't seem so tall when he was sitting down.

'Now Tim,' he said, 'tell me. Did you open the cage?'

'Yes sir,' said Tim.

'Why?' he asked.

'I wanted to bring him out to the woods,' Tim said. 'So that he would get well, and Putrid wouldn't torture him.'

Tim told him about Putrid.

'I see,' said the Inspector.

'Samson is not well,' said Tim. 'You should have seen him. He wouldn't roar nor nothing. And he should have. He should have eaten Putrid. But he didn't do nothing. Just sat when he stuck things into him and pulled his tail and everything. You see, Samson should be in the woods to get well.'

'I see,' said the Inspector. He took up the telephone and called a number into it. He tapped with a pencil on the desk as he waited. His eyes were hard. Tim was frightened again.

'That you, Joe?' he asked. 'Yes, it's me. I want you down here in about ten minutes. Bring your bag of tricks with you. Yes, I'll explain to you then. It's urgent.'

He put down the phone. He pressed a button and started to write lines on a sheet of paper. Another policeman came in.

'Here,' he said. 'Go to the J P down the road and get him to sign that.' The policeman went.

'All right, Tim,' said the Inspector, 'come on and we'll go out and wait for Joe.'

'What are you going to do with me?' Tim asked. 'Will I have to go to jail?'

The Inspector looked at him for a moment, then put his hand on his head.

'No, Tim,' he said. 'No jail. On the other hand, no medal either. They don't give out medals for the kind of good deed you do. Come on.' They went out. The Inspector opened the door of a car and put Tim in before him. There was a bulky red-faced man behind the wheel.

'Hello, Joe,' said the Inspector. 'This is Tim, a friend of mine.'

'Hello, Tim,' said Joe. 'Glad the Inspector has decent friends for a change.'

The policeman came breathless then, shoved in the paper through the window.

'He made no trouble about it?' the Inspector asked.

'Not a bit,' said the policeman, laughing. 'Said he'd sign an order to burn the circus as well.'

The Inspector laughed.

'Fine. All right, Joe.'

The car moved away.

'What's all this about a lion?' Joe asked. 'Everybody is talking about it.'

'That's the lion you are going to see,' said the Inspector. He explained to Tim. 'Joe is a doctor of animals, Tim. He cares for animals, like a doctor cares for people.'

Tim was interested.

'Oh,' he said. 'Will you make Samson well?'

'He will, Tim, don't worry,' said the Inspector.

Joe was a bit bewildered, but kept silent under the appeal of the Inspector's wink.

The car stopped outside the circus entrance. The town had returned to normal.

'You stay here, Tim,' said the Inspector. 'We won't be long.'

They left him. Tim opened a window. He could smell the circus. He didn't want to go in there again.

Joe was looking at Samson.

'What do you think?' the Inspector asked.

'I'm afraid so,' said Joe.

'You wait here,' said the Inspector.

He found the owner. He presented him with the signed order.

'You can't do that,' he protested. 'It's illegal. There's nothing wrong with him. Just because some crazy kid let him out. That's no reason. Here, Alphonsus. Come here. He knows. He keeps them fed. You know that Samson is all right, isn't he? Isn't Samson all right?'

'Strong as a lion,' said Alphonsus, chuckling.

'You are Putrid,' said the Inspector suddenly to Alphonsus. He thought how vivid had been the boy's description of him.

'You're a dirty little sadistic bastard,' he said, 'and if a lion doesn't tear you to pieces some day, some honest man will kick your puddens out.'

Putrid's mouth was open in astonishment.

The owner protested.

'Here,' he said. 'You can't say things like that.'

'You keep that fella away from your animals,' said the Inspector and walked away from them.

Joe was at the cage. He was putting away a syringe. Samson was lying on the floor of the cage, his legs stiffened straight out from him. His chest was not rising.

They looked at the body of the lion.

'He should have been destroyed years ago,' Joe said.

'Poor devil,' said the Inspector. He put his hand through the bars of the cage, rested it on the body of Samson.

'That's from Tim, Samson,' he said, and then they walked back to the car. They got in.

They could sense the silence of the boy.

'What happened?' he asked.

Joe started the car.

The Inspector put his arm around Tim's shoulders.

'Samson is gone back to the woods, Tim,' he said. 'You watch. One time maybe when you are playing in that wood, you might see Samson standing in the sunlight.'

'Resting on the soft leaves,' said Tim eagerly.

'That's right,' said the Inspector.

Arcady

E. L. KENNEDY

'Where do you live?' asked the school inspector.

'In Arcady,' said I.

Mrs Conlan frowned at me behind his back, and I remembered to make it into a sentence the way she is always telling me.

'I live in Arcady,' I said to him.

'Where is that?' he asked me.

'Arcady is an old factory down by the river,' I said to him, 'but it is in flats now. We live in the first flat at the head of the stairs.'

'And who are we?' he asked me.

'Daddy and Mammy and Agnes and Bertie and Mria and Alec and Doreen and Mervyn and Hector and George and wee James,' I said to him.

'Could you describe Arcady,' he asked me, 'so that I would know it if I saw it?'

'Well,' I said to him, 'it is three storeys high and you go round the side if you want to get into the lower flats. They have two rooms, one behind the other. But ours is up the outside steps. You go up the steps to a balcony and four front doors are on it, ours, and Lyle's, and an empty flat, and Pettigrew's. The upper flats have four rooms, two up and two down. The steps are cement and the balcony is cement, with an iron railing. On wet days the balcony is covered with shallow puddles.'

'Very good,' he said, and asked Vera Gorman where she lives.

She told him her daddy works in Belfast and her mammy has a shop and a post office, and her aunt is a staff nurse, and they live in a white house on the Belfast Road. Vera is an only child. It is a pity of her.

The inspector talked a while to Mrs Conlan, and then asked us to write a short description of our families.

Well, how are you, Burke! There are twelve in our house, I thought to myself, so I would not be a quarter finished in the time. He was watching Alice Todd. She has it easy, nothing at home but her mother and brother Don and a canary and her daddy.

I thought I'd better get cracking. That is what Daddy says, get cracking.

My daddy is a tall man with dark hair and eyes and a small moustache. He is thin and brown and was in the western desert in the war. His best friend is Shamus McCann who keeps pigeons and fishes in the river if the police are not watching him. Daddy wears a blue shirt and navy jeans and a big leather belt with rejimentle badges on it, and black tough shoes or wellingtons. He still has his battledress jacket from the war and he wears it when it is cold. He is the best darts player in Guinan's and the best Daddy in Arcady. He is buying a lorry to go into the road-haulage business.

My mammy is very pretty and she has her hair bleached and she says she weighs twelve stone but I don't believe it. She is not very tall and has a good figure and can cook very well. She gives me threepence on Saturdays for scrubbing the kitchen floor and I get three toffee chews and give her one. She always chooses the liquorice one.

I am the eldest. I am twelve. Agnes is eleven and wears glasses and is a tell-tale. She is not in the same class as me and I am glad. It would be torture. Bertie is ten and not a lot of use. He is supposed to get sticks from Harper's Planting for our fire, and he forgets, and my mammy is waiting maybe an hour for the sticks before I have to go and get some to keep the fire in. Mria is nine and there is a joke about her and Bertie being Irish twins. She is home, sick. She has a bad throat this three weeks, and Mammy does not know what is wrong with her. Doreen and Alec are really twins. They are eight. My daddy says it is a pity there are two of them, because he could lick either one single-handed, but he is outnubmered. I mean outnumbered. This is only a joke. He never hits any of us, even on Saturday nights when he has been in Guinan's. Mervyn is seven and George is nearly five. We thought Mervyn would never learn to read but the nurse came to school and found out he could not see, so now he has glasses and can see the very best. He is very fond of reading. George cannot read yet. Hector is between Mervyn and George but he does not go to school because he is not well. He is six, but George has more sense than him. Daddy says we will all have to take great care of Hector because he does not know down from up, or hot from cold, and likely never will. My mammy says she has two babies, Hector and wee James. But wee James is thriving like a gosling and nearly two years old, and is so quick on his feet you can't watch him. He has blue eyes and a pink face and a fluff of white hair, and Mammy is always scared in case he gets out and falls in the river. Once Hector . . .

'Time up,' said the inspector.

I was not near finished. And it was three o'clock. That was the shortest afternoon I ever mind.

*

I hoped Daddy had got the lorry by now. He says there is lots of work about for an intelligent man with a lorry, doing flits for people and carting stuff for the farmers that are too busy to do it themselves, and he could cart peat from the Far Moss and sell it round the town. My daddy is working at the labour exchange. He only goes three times a week but he gets paid the full week just the same. He says there is little to do but stand, and Mammy laughs at that. He always says if he could get a job for the other three days he would be on the pig's back, but Mammy says, 'Six or nothing, you know you got into a quare row the last time. You nearly got jail, and left me a grass-widow.'

A grass-widow is what you are when your husband runs away. Mrs Conlan's husband did not run away, she put him out. He would not work or give her any money for the house. She is my teacher. He was a commercial traveller and I did not like him. He said something to Mammy one day she was coming into Arcady past the bungalow, so she set down wee James on the ditch and went and warmed both his ears, then came back and picked up wee James and walked on. I was with her.

I wished I was home. Mammy was sick in the morning but she would not let me stay at home. I could have kept Hector and wee James out of her road for a while, and redd up the kitchen, and got sticks, and emptied the bucket. And I could have taken a look at the new people in the cottage. They only came the night before, late, and I had not laid eyes on them yet. I wanted to go over and tell them that their well is condemned, and to get their water from the pump at the steps, the same as we do.

The last one to live in the cottage was old Barney Hake. His name was not Hake, but that was what we called him. I never heard him called anything else. Mammy would not let us go near him, for she said he should be in the asylum. That is where he is now. He ran out one night in his shirt, all the way over the Stock Bridge in his bare feet, and it raining, to the Belfast Road. He said he would walk to Belfast to see Rangers play Linfield, and that he would split the first one that tried to stop him. Old Joe Cooper ran for the rector, and my daddy phoned for the police but they would not believe him. Shamus McCann ran after Barney and he and Dermot Ryan caught him at the bus stop. They told him that he was going the wrong way, that they were for Belfast too and would see him right. Dermot put his coat on him, and Barney let him, then they kept him safe until the doctor came in his car and took them all to the asylum. When Shamus and Dermot came back, they were not laughing. They said it was a pity of Barney, we might all end that way, and where was Old Joe Cooper.

With that, Old Joe Cooper came up the steps and asked them how Barney was, so they told him he was under a sedative, and Old Joe said he did not know what the world was coming to, and that Barney should have a bit of sense. It was funny to hear because Barney Hake is seventy-six but Old Joe is over ninety.

Mammy says Old Joe will never die because he is hand-made. One Saturday he ate six sausages for his tea and he was not well, so Mrs McFarland ran for Mammy as well as she was able, and Mammy ran for Mrs Conlan, and she phoned for the doctor.

It was Dr Emily who came and said, 'Put him in the car and I'll take him to hospital just in case. Will you take your hand off my leg you saucy old man you before I belt you one,' and she drove off.

My mammy laughed so much she had an accident going up the steps. But Mrs Conlan did not think it was funny. Old Joe Cooper was none the worse and came back the next day on the bus and said they were good to him and the doctor had a grand chassy. Then he ate three more sausages, just to show them, he said.

That was last year, though. It was after that that he ran for the rector for Barney.

About Barney going to the asylum Old Joe said, 'What would you expect, the man lives on wee sups of tea and bread and jam and would not know a square male if he saw one. If we had him at Lady Smith or Maggers Fonteen he would have got a hungering that would have lasted him to this day. Dammit, I never pass a horse without wondering how it would eat if there was a sudden famine.'

'Tell your uncle Dan,' said Daddy to Dermot, 'to keep that brown horse of his well out of Joe's road, for he might just take a snap at it going past.'

They all laughed, but I was glad Barney was away because I was afraid of him. He followed Agnes and me down the Water Walks one day, and would not let us by him when we wanted to go home. I could have got by but Agnes would not have been fast enough.

I was so scared I was sick, but I shouted, 'There's my daddy!' He turned to see where and we ran past him, and ran and ran until we got to the open space past his cottage, and then we could not run anymore. Agnes started to laugh and I started to cry, but we did not know why we were so frightened. He did not do anything except stretch out his arms across the path, so as not to let us pass. We had to tell Mammy because she wanted to know what I was crying for. Then she said never to go near him, and to run if we saw him, and not to get cornered, and to jump in the river sooner then let him catch us.

'But we would drown,' said Agnes.

'I do not mean in the deep part,' said Mammy, 'just the stretch at his cottage. You could walk in the river from there to the rock at the back of Finlay's and it would not come over your shoulders unless there was a flood. But don't for God's sake go in anywhere else, especially below the Beetling-house for it is forty feet there. In fact don't go near the Beetling-house. I bathed in this river when I was not any bigger than you and I know every foot of it. I learned to swim here.'

'Why do you not swim yet?' asked Agnes.

'Have I time?' said Mammy.

It was now ten past three and still a mile to Arcady. I wondered had Mrs Conlan the car with her. I thought that if I offered to carry her books for her she might have offered us a lift, not all of us, just Agnes and me. The boys and the twins were already home, I saw them go.

There is no place at Mrs Conlan's bungalow where she can turn the car and if she drives into the garage the car will be facing the wrong way in the morning, so she usually drives down into Arcady and out again, and reverses into the garage. This is because she cannot reverse and make a turn coming into the garage from the Pack Bridge Road. I do not know why, she just can't.

Just then she came by, and, come here, she did offer us a lift.

'My mammy is not very well,' said I. 'We are very glad of a lift. Thank you very much, Mrs Conlan.'

'Indeed, I don't know how she manages with you all,' she said. 'Are you warm enough with that window open? Good gracious, you are like ice. Agnes, reach your sister that yellow cardigan from the back seat. You had better keep it, it suits you and it is too tight for me. It must have shrunk in the wash.'

The cardigan was very thick and fuzzy, it felt lovely on my arms. The school is warm enough, but short sleeves are no good to walk home in, even if it takes only twenty minutes. Mammy says it is only coming in out of the cold that makes me cough but Daddy says I need flannel on my chest, so the cardigan will do instead. It is the same colour as the kingcups at the side of the river in the month of May.

The new people were in the cottage. There was smoke coming from the chimney, it was like the one in Mervyn's new Reader. And a soldier was hagging sticks on the front path. But I had no time to stop. I was up the steps and into our house in a flash. Mammy was sitting at the fire, only the fire was out and Hector had knocked over the bucket, it was lying on its side and all he had done in it was soaking into the floor. Wee James was in his cot, trying to get out and crying.

'Where are the rest of you?' asked Mammy.

'They are coming,' I said, and grabbed a bucket and went for water. I had to scrub the floor at once, and get sticks too if I could. The floor-cloth was all holes and slimy, it was so skiddy that I could hardly wring it out and the smell was awful. The nurse wants us to let Hector go to the Hospital School. She says they could teach him to keep clean and we could see him once a week, but Mammy says she could not stand not knowing how he was getting on.

The pump has a handle on a wheel, and it took all my weight to swing it, it is more like a mangle than a pump.

When I got in again I threw my good yellow cardigan up on the high line in the kitchen, so that it would not get dirty, and washed and wiped at the floor till it was near dry. It is a wood floor and whatever is spilled on it sinks into it, the first hot fire we have will bring out the smell again.

Then we had to get sticks.

Mammy said she would not come with us because wee James was crying and Mria was coughing and Hector needed changing. I knew from Mammy's face that she had a head-ache. She gets real bad ones sometimes, fit to split a paving-stone, she says.

Harper's Planting is not far from the house, up the lane out of Arcady, and over to the right behind Mrs Conlan's bun-galow, about half-way to the Pack Bridge Road. Mr Harper said we can take all we can get of the trees, even cut them down, because he wants to put cattle there and it is not safe for them until we have cleared out the dead branches and stumps. On fine evenings Daddy and Bertie take a bag and a saw and cut a bag of blocks. But Daddy won't let any of us have the saw if he is not there so on that day we were only able to get small stuff. There are still fifteen trees left, one very big and four medium, and ten little ones off which you can break bits if you are determined. The little trees will hardly burn at all though, they have smooth grey bark. The others have rough bark with grey moss on it and they burn like fun, but you would need the saw because they won't break.

Bertie is not as old as me or as big so he had to do what I said. He would have needed to, he would have got nothing done if he did not because he is as lazy as sheugh water.

At the last we had quite a big bunch of branches gathered and tied with an old bit of rope, and we were pulling and heaving this way and that way, trying to get it to the lane, but it was catching in all the stumps and snags hidden in the grass.

I would love to be rich and order in a load of coal like Mrs Conlan.

The coalman comes to the school and says, 'Any coal, mam?'

She gives him the key of her coalshed and says, 'You may put in a ton, Harry.'

So he puts it in and shoves the coalshed key through her letterbox, then she gets it when she goes home at three o'clock.

This time we had a long drag of it, because we had got all the near branches long ago. We had to go right to the back of the Planting and pull all we got right across it. It was nearly dark and the wee ones were on ahead with the twins, taking the little bits they got, but Bertie and Agnes and I could not get the bundle of branches over the ditch. Two men we don't know came by with guns.

One handed the other his gun and said, 'Would you let me give you a hand with that or you will be here all night. Whose kids are you anyway?'

Bertie told him and he said nothing, just gave that big bunch of branches a heave. It flew over the ditch and hit the lane. The rope broke but he tied it again.

Then he said, 'Night, kids,' and went after the other man.

We were home in two minutes and Mammy had a wee fire going and the pan on. Fried bread is lovely when you are all cold and scratched. I could not wear my good yellow cardigan to get sticks, it would have got torn to bits on the branches.

'You got on well the night,' said Mammy. 'Where did yous get that lot? That'll keep the life in us a while longer.'

'That's the last,' said Bertie. 'Unless me and my da was to saw some. Maybe we could take a tree. It would last us a quare while.'

'Sure you could never take a tree! How would you get it sawed?' said my mammy.

'We could do it rightly,' said Bertie. 'But my da would have to cut it down first,' he added.

It was only to get using the saw and my daddy not there at the time, that was all that was in his head, for I know him. Once Bertie had the sawing of a tree he would lose notion of the job. He always does. But what's the use of talking.

And my daddy was not home yet.

I screwed my head round to see what time it was, because our clock does not go except when it is lying on its side. It was after six o'clock.

'Where in under God can he be?' said my mammy. 'And Mria worse, I wish he was here this minute to go for the doctor. Bertie, you'll have to go or we will miss the night surgery. Write this down,' she said to me. ' "Mria has a bad throat and a cough and would you please come over after surgery, yours truly, Ethel." ' She threw a coat over her head and shoulders, and said to Bertie, 'I'll convoy you across the Stick Bridge, then you run to the road, and don't stop to think. I want you to stop George Harvey's car and give him the note to give to Billy Wiseman to give to the doctor. If you miss him you may walk it, so shift yourself, I haven't the price of a bus after four loaves from Matt Edgar.'

When she had gone Agnes washed the dishes and I cleaned Hector. He had slobbered gravy all over his face and hands, sometimes I think he doesn't know the road to his mouth. The nappies on the high line were dry so I took them down, then washed out the four in the basin and rinsed them at the pump.

I had to fetch more water too because Mammy would have to bath Hector and wee James when she got back. My hands were so cold I could hardly wring the nappies. She has a hard time of it with us all.

'Never marry,' she often says to me. 'It is cutting a stick to beat yourself with.'

'Come on, Ethel,' said my daddy once when he heard her say it, 'you enjoy yourself rightly at times.'

She started to laugh at him and said, 'Aye, so!' very sarcastically.

When I came back with the two buckets the wee ones were just ready to start a bit of codding, but I had to make them learn their lessons for the next day. Every night that week Bertie was away out to swing in an old tyre tied to a rope on Barney's tree, but he could not do that now even if he was back, for the cottage had people in it and they would not like it, forbye he would be looking in their windows and cheering and yelling. He is mad about aeroplanes and pretends he is flying one and shooting down Germans. Daddy was through the war and he says he never saw a German, only Italians. He says they ran as if they were reared on senna pods when they heard General Montgomery was coming with the desert rats. He was a desert rat and he is proud of it.

Mammy came back, shivering and rubbing her arms. Her jersey has short sleeves now because it had big holes in the elbows so she cut off the sleeves just above the holes to make it look civilized.

'Is it dark?' asked George. He is like a wee old man. I do not think he knows what dark is.

'It's dark all right,' said Mammy. 'Dear but this is cosy now we have a bit of fire. I think it's freezing. The moon's all crined [1] in wee, and you can hardly hear the river. It's very like a night you would have snow. Where the devil is your da and why isn't he home? I declare this is scandalous.'

1. Shrunk.

'Is Bertie all right to come back by himself?' said I. 'Sure if he misses the Stick Bridge he'll be in the river before he knows.'

'Not him,' said Mammy, 'I tied my apron to the far end of the handrail. He's to gather it up and bring it with him when he's coming back. Take off that kettle, it's boiling. Where are the dishes, or did you do them when you got my back turned?'

'I did them,' said Agnes, 'I did the dishes and she did not.'

'Well she was not idle,' said my mammy to her, for she knew it was me did the nappies and fetched water and kept the fire up and started the wee ones at their lessons. 'Go on, ye boys ye!' she said to the wee ones. 'See who is finished first and I'll hear you your tables.'

'I haven't any tables,' said Mervyn.

'Never mind,' she said, 'I will teach you some and then you will be able for them when you do get them. It pays to be smart.'

It was time Agnes and I started our tables because we are learning hard ones. Agnes is at parts of a pound and I am at per cents. I would rather do per cents than parts of a pound for I have done them twice and I don't know yet what one eighth is, a twelfth, or a sixteenth.

'Hurry up you two,' said Mammy to us, 'and I will wash your hair and you can dry it at the fire. It's a wonder you're not lousy. You're for it the next time, Doreen, I think I'll cut yours and give you a with-it look.'

'I'm sure you'll not,' said Doreen.

'What did I hear you say?' asked Mammy.

'Nothing,' said Doreen.

'That would need to be the truth,' said Mammy. 'Do you think I need a licence to cut your hair, or maybe an Act of Parliament?'

Doreen said nothing and minded her business, Mammy was just waiting for the chance to clash her ears if she was cheeky.

Bertie came in with Mammy's apron all rolled up and threw it to her. 'I got him,' he said. 'Can I go round to Dennis Barkley's?'

'You can not,' said Mammy. 'Sit down and do your ecker,[1] are you mad?'

She was asking Mervyn his spellings and I was asking Doreen hers, but Hector started to yell and shout. Mammy had to take him on her knee and hold him with one hand while she asked Mervyn his spellings, looking past Hector at the book in her other hand. Hector did not want her to do this and started to slap at her face, so that she had to twist her head away. The rest of us would not get away with what he gets away with, but Hector is not just right.

'Would one of you strip wee James,' she said, 'before he falls asleep in a heap like a wee pup.'

Wee James was as cross as a fitch and it had to be Bertie or nobody, he is Bertie's boy and Bertie could do rightly without him. But at last he was in his bed and everybody felt the relief, for he fell asleep the minute he was in. Mammy could start bathing Hector at the fire. Hector was well enough content because now she was attending to him and nobody else. Then she put him to bed too.

Bertie had to learn to spell expedition for the next day and he could not, he got it wrong every time.

Mammy asked him, 'What does it mean anyway?'

'Crossing the Stick Bridge in the dark,' he said, 'that's an expedition.'

We all laughed.

'You tell that to the master tomorrow,' said Mammy drily.

'It is a journey that is not too simple,' said Bertie. 'You might not make it.'

'Well, good for you,' she said. 'You deserve to know how to spell it. Come on and we'll have another bash at it, it can't be that hard if you know what it is.'

By the time she had finished with us we could all spell it, even Mervyn, by shouting it out in chorus. Of course I could spell it anyway. I was kept in for not knowing it last week, that's why. Mrs Conlan is brave and easy if you don't under-

1. Work.

stand the sums, but she says any fool can spell. It is just learned off like a parrot, and if a parrot can, you can. We are all smarter than parrots except Hector, so we had it off in no time.

'Would you look out,' said Mammy, 'and see is your father coming at all, or is he staying the night with his rich friends.'

This is a joke. When he is late home he always says he was being entertained by his rich friends. It is just a saying. One night Mammy cried and said she would have the truth from him if she had to peel him like an onion, and he laughed so much he had to lie down. He woke us up twice that night, laughing at what she had said to him.

'What are you doing,' she said to him, and the clock struck four.

'Laughing, what else,' he said. 'It's a great life if you don't weaken.'

'You fool you,' said she.

When I opened the door to see if Daddy was coming there was a noise in the lane so I waited to see if it was the doctor's car, but it is bigger and had no lights. It came down as if the driver knew the place and it ran round the pump and swung till it was facing the mouth of the lane. I thought it was a lorry. A man jumped down out of the front and slammed the door, and here, wasn't it my daddy.

'You got it,' I said to him.

'I got it,' he said to me. 'There'll be no holding us now. Ethel,' he said, 'I got the truck, fifteen pounds and a jack thrown in. It's not much to look at but there's life in it yet, like somebody else I could name. Come out till yous see her.'

It was dark and cold but we all came out except Mria and Hector and wee James.

'Well, she needs new tyres but that's a detail,' said Daddy, kicking the wheels. 'Sure she's as sound as you like. I've a bargain here, she should have been eighty but he's going to Marrafelt and has no yard now to keep her in.'

With that the doctor drove up, and it was Dr John, not Dr

Emily. Before he could speak my mammy had us all into the house, except Daddy, who wanted to fix something on the lorry.

'I thought there had been an accident,' said the doctor. 'Where is the invalid?'

'It's Mria,' said Mammy. 'She is in her bed. Where else would she be?'

'Missus, dear,' said Dr John, 'would you send a wheen of these wee weans to bed so that I can see the one that's not well.'

Well the boys went up, but Agnes and I could not because we sleep in the low back room with Mria.

I shouted out to Daddy, 'Do you want your tea?'

He said, 'You bet! So that's what's wrong with me!'

When he came in his hands were black with oil from the lorry, but luckily I had the kettle hot and he could have a wash. I had two big slices of fried bread for him and a cup of tea wet. There was not any milk left, but he never takes milk in it anyway.

'Keep her in bed,' said the doctor, 'and don't let the others near her. Have they had their diphtheria shots?'

'Why, has Mria got it?' asked Mammy, sounding scared.

'She's got a bad throat,' said the doctor, 'and that's one reason why.' He nodded at the bucket we have to have for Hector because he does not know the way down to the closet.

Till George started school he could take him down, but since then Hector will not go out of the house without Mammy, so she just has to let him do it in the bucket.

'Is that right?' said Mammy. 'Well, I do try and train him but he is very odd lately, he will not do anything he does not want to do. If the rest tried it I could skelp them, but what can I do with him? Lately he will not go out the door without a roaring match, even with the rest for company.'

'I have told you what you ought to do about it,' said Dr John. 'If you won't you won't, but you might think of the poor child. He will be warm and fed and kindly treated. You know quite well, Ethel, the Priory is not a jail, and he is such a risk to the others in this crowded house. Sore throats are the least part of it. Just think whiles who will look after him when you are not able to. Keep that Mria in bed and give her no food, only warm drinks. And get those tablets tonight, and see if she can't get some sleep.' And away he went.

'Have you two shillings?' asked Daddy.

'I have not,' said Mammy. 'Are you mad? Where would I get two shillings?'

'Singing in the Fair Hill,' said Daddy.

But Mammy did not laugh. 'I know you want it for the bus,' she said, 'but I have not got it, and that is God's honest truth.'

'Then the child'll get no tablets this night,' said Daddy. 'There is no use in walking in because the chemists will be shut by then,' and he ate up the rest of his fried bread.

I had hoped he would leave a bit because I was still hungry.

'Would you run up to Mrs Conlan's,' Mammy said to me, 'and ask her would she lend me two shillings.'

'Don't you dare,' said Daddy, 'I will ask Dermot in a minute. If I went down now I'd catch him in the middle of "Z-Cars" and he would not answer me till it was over, and then maybe say he hadn't it . . . No, it would be no use.'

'Away quick to Mrs Conlan's,' said Mammy to me. 'Tell her I'll pay her it back on Friday. Run or it will be too late for you to catch the bus.'

It was very dark in the lane and I was afraid to walk in case something caught my tail, so I ran all the way.

Her door is painted black with a shiny brass letterbox and knocker. I knocked and knocked before she heard me. She had the television on, for I could hear the voices in 'Z-Cars' and Fancy Smith was talking. I love him.

At last she opened the door and said, 'Mercy me, is that you and I never heard you. What is it you want, child? Come in out of the cold this minute.'

Her living-room is lovely, with a green sweet of furniture and thick curtains and a television and a wee table with a big glass vase full of pompous grass and a green rug with a pattern on it at the fire, and the fire was piled up with big lumps of coal and plenty of slack. I could hardly tell her about the two shillings for looking at her pictures, one is the Virgin Mary because Mrs Conlan is a Catholic and the other is a woman in a long white dress and umbrella in a garden with flowerbeds.

In the middle of it Mrs Conlan gave a yell, 'My oven!' She ran into the kitchen, tore open the oven door, snatched out an oven soda, a little bit burnt, and an apple pie. A lovely smell of hot apples and sugar came out of the oven and she said to me: 'I suppose you would not say No to a piece of pie?'

'I would not, indeed, thank you very much, Mrs Conlan,' I said, 'but I have to go to the town for Mria's tablets, or none of us will get a wink of sleep. She has to have them and if I miss the bus the chemists will be shut by the time I have walked it.'

'Well, it's a mercy you came here,' she said, getting out a plate and a spoon, 'because I am going into the town in about ten minutes. You can come with me in the car. So you will still have time to eat your pie.'

'I have no prescription with me,' said I, 'I will run and get it.'

'Eat your pie,' she said. 'You can get it when I turn the car. You will have to take the bus home, dear, so here is the money.'

'Sure I might get a lift,' I said.

'Don't you dare,' she said, very seriously. 'You never know who is driving up that road at night. You are never to take a lift with anybody you don't know, do you hear?'

'That is what Mammy always says,' I told her.

Well, as soon as I had finished my share of the pie, she got the car out and we sailed down into Arcady in quare style. I got the prescription off Mammy, and we arrived in the town in just a minute or two. Mrs Conlan reached me a half-crown and told me to be sure and catch the bus, and not go roaming the town because it was coming on to snow and I had no coat with me.

Mrs Conlan knows rightly that I have no coat because I am the biggest and Agnes has mine and Doreen has Agnes's, but she lets on she doesn't know. I can get on the best without one. I would like one fine, but a coat costs pounds, and shoes are more important. Mammy says she will get me a coat the first chance she has, and I know she will. It will be easier now my daddy has got the lorry at last.

In the car I asked Mrs Conlan how you spell Shamus and it is not spelled like that at all, it is Seumas or Seamus, I forget which.

Gypsy

SAM McBRATNEY

Gypsy came into the house before Danny Murray was born. She hung on the wall above the battered old piano with the yellow keys. Danny didn't like her cross face when he was little. Sometimes when he did his piano practice he climbed up on the stool and turned the picture to the wall so that she couldn't listen.

Gypsy had thin red lips under a crooked big nose. Her eyelids were always half-closed in a sly sort of way – as if to hide what she was really thinking. The pearls round her neck looked like blobs of paint from close-up, but when you stepped back they caught the light, and glowed. Like magic, really, Gypsy was so real that Danny used to wonder whether she was still alive somewhere in the world.

One day Catherine Parr from down the street came into

the house and she said that Gypsy's lips were red because she ate poisonous berries. She stuck out her tongue at Gypsy and she made Danny do the same.

When Danny was nine Gypsy got him into trouble. He climbed up on the piano stool and tried to give her a shave with his Daddy's razor and wobbling brush, but his mother came into the room at the wrong moment, and caught him in the act.

'Oh my glory!' she said. Mountains of creamy lather stood out from Gypsy's chin like snowcapped mountains on a map of the world. An avalanche of snow had blocked up her long, Roman nose.

'Danny Murray! Oh, I will murder you, you bad article. Brian – come you in here this minute, he's shaving *Gypsy*!'

His Daddy arrived, breathless, and did some staring at Gypsy's altered face.

'What are you playing at? Are you stupid? The only thing in the house that could be worth a fortune, and what do *you* do with it? Give it a blasted *shave*!'

And so Danny found himself driven up the stairs by the flat of his father's hand. That was the first time he realized that Gypsy might not be just any old picture. In some mysterious way, maybe she was worth something.

About this time Dr Moore began to call at the house to examine Danny's father, who wasn't feeling well. During one of these visits the doctor happened to notice Gypsy.

'Mrs Murray,' he said, peering through his bushy eyebrows, 'I have to remark on that dark-skinned beauty on your wall. Now that's what I call a proper picture! Where did you get her – did you pick her up cheap at one of the auctions?'

'No, sure we've had that for years,' said Danny's mother. 'Maggie O'Brien and her man lit out for Canada and they auctioned all their stuff at the front door. My grandfather bought the picture and her mangle for two and six.'

Dr Moore smiled, and repeated, 'Two and six!' as he turned the painting over in his hands. 'Pity it's not signed. But look at this canvas, I'd say this wasn't done by one of your weekend artists. Did you ever think of selling her?'

'Ah no,' said his mother, turning a bit red. 'Brian says we couldn't sell our luck.'

'Well now – give me the first refusal,' said Dr Moore, who aimed a massive wink at Danny as he put his stethoscope on Gypsy's chest and pretended to be deafened by the noise of her insides.

After that Danny's parents talked about Gypsy as if she was money in the bank. His Daddy used to say that he was going to sell Gypsy and buy a yacht and keep it in the harbour at Ballyholme. His mother wanted a house in the country with chickens and a goat. 'How Will We Spend Gypsy' became a favourite family game. Then, when Danny turned eleven, his father died, and of course everything changed.

The Headmaster said special prayers for Danny in Assembly one morning. People were sorry for him because his Daddy had gone away to Heaven, and indeed, he was sorry for himself and for his Mummy. It was a long time before she did many of her ordinary things about the house, such as play the old piano in the living room. Then one day she played and made Danny sing that stupid song about Paddy McGinty's goat, and Danny felt good. They bought a black labrador pup and they had trouble teaching it not to widdle everywhere.

Danny noticed another change that came over his life at this time: there was no money to spend now that they had to live on what his Mummy earned. Sometimes he remembered the day when he bought three bars of Caramilk in the sweetie shop and ate them one after another on the way to school.

'You are one greedy spoiled pig, Danny Murray,' Catherine Parr had told him, just because he only gave her two squares.

Now, times had changed. Catherine Parr was able to go on the school trip to Brittany, but Danny's mother sat down and cried when he told her what it would cost. Even when she became Manageress of the laundry where she worked on the

Newtownards Road, still she complained that he grew too fast and ranted about the awful things he could do to a pair of shoes.

'I am going to buy you a pair of wooden Dutch clogs, Danny Murray,' she used to say.

His mother was very friendly with the woman who owned the local fruit, vegetable and flower shop. This lady, Miss Finlay, gave Danny a job after school on Fridays and all day Saturdays. He spent most of the time sweeping the floors and making up delivery boxes. One afternoon Danny was wrapping an old newspaper round six big earthy leeks when an interesting headline caught his eye:

Fortune In The Attic

A County Antrim farmer learned yesterday that the painting found in his attic could be worth as much as £80,000.

'I'm only flabbergasted,' he told our reporter. 'It's been up there for years, I nearly threw it out. I don't even like it, you know – I like pictures with horses in them.'

When asked what he was going to do with his windfall, Mr Cowan said, 'Enjoy it!'

Danny began to think. If his Mummy had £80,000 she wouldn't have to scrimp and save or worry about the price of shoes. He thought of Gypsy's sly, hooded eyes; of the fine, strong jaw he'd once tried to shave; of the pearls round her neck and how they seemed to glow from within if the light was right. Only a good artist could paint like that, even Dr Moore had said so.

How much, he wondered, was Gypsy really worth?

'Daniel Murray,' called Miss Finlay from the front of the shop, 'what's keeping those leeks – are you growing them, or what?'

That very evening, Danny made a point of sitting with his mother while she did some ironing. From time to time she wet the clothes with vapour from a plastic spray.

'Mummy.'

'U-huh?'

'Miss Finlay says if you take a picture into a shop near the City Hall, they'll tell you what it's worth.'

'Is that a fact, Danny.'

'What would you buy if we sold Gypsy?'

For a moment or two, no answer came. His mother squeezed a squirt of misty water over the collar of a shirt.

'I couldn't sell Gypsy, I've had her since I was a wee girl.'

'But if you *did* sell her, what would you buy?'

'A cuckoo clock!' said his mother, aiming a squirt of water at him. 'Now run away out and play.'

Two more weeks went by, bringing the end of term and the start of the Easter holidays. Danny was bored in the house on his own. Most of his best friends were away with the school to Brittany and it didn't help him to think what a great time they must all be having over there. On Tuesday afternoon he came back from walking the dog in the Ormeau Park, and made a decision that set his blood racing.

He gently lifted Gypsy from the wall, put her into a large carrier bag, and caught a bus into town.

The journey into the centre of Belfast seemed to take about two minutes, for Danny's mind would not be still when he thought of what might happen in the next half hour. Goodbye Mr Scrimp and Mr Save. His mother might even give up her job! They could both fly out to see Uncle Robert in New Zealand or buy a house in the country and keep chickens and a car. Danny could think of dozens of ways of spending Gypsy, even if she wasn't worth quite as much as eighty thousand pounds.

He walked down Wellington Place and stood outside the shop with his heart beating like an engine, urging him on. His blood quickened, but his mind refused to be driven and he could not move. His mother would have a fit if she saw him right now! Danny closed his eyes and swallowed, thinking nervously how this was a bit like getting into the cold sea at Millisle. He took the plunge and went right in.

He was the only customer in the cool and very quiet gallery. The central area of the shop was fairly dim compared with the walls, which were illuminated by strips of fluorescent lighting. Some of the pictures hanging there were so huge that they made Gypsy look like a puny little thing – and to his amazement, Danny saw some very fancy carpets hanging on the walls.

Funny place to keep your carpets, he was thinking when a voice spoke.

'Yes? What do you want?'

The man who now approached wore a shabby Aran jumper. Using his fingers as a rake, he shifted his long grey hair away from his face.

'I've got a picture here,' said Danny. 'Could you tell me please if it's worth anything?'

'Another one. All right, let's take a look at it.'

The man fitted glasses over his nose as he carried Gypsy a little closer to the window. He tapped the canvas with his fingernail and turned her over to examine the back just as Dr Moore had done all those years ago. Danny wanted to tell him some interesting things about his picture – how her name was Gypsy, that they'd had her for years and years, how she was supposed to be lucky – but he didn't have time. The man whipped the glasses off his face.

'This painting has no commercial value whatsoever. The frame might fetch a penny or two if it was competently restored, but the work itself . . .? Most likely a student's copy. No.'

Danny accepted back his picture without speaking. No commercial value. A copy. That final word fell on his ears like a blow – No. He swallowed hard, gathering his courage, wanting to strike back.

'But . . . didn't you see her pearls?'

'I saw her pearls.'

Gypsy. How it destroyed him to think she wasn't even worth a cuckoo clock.

'But how do you *know*? How do you know she isn't worth anything?'

'Look, son,' said the man, 'what's your name?'

'Danny Murray.'

'Right. Suppose that twenty or thirty women lined up outside this shop and one of them was your mother. And they all shouted "Danny Murray" one after another. Do you think you'd know your mother's voice, could you pick it out from the others?'

'Probably.'

'Well that's how it is with paintings. You know your mother's voice when you hear it because you're an expert on that topic. A great and valuable painting is like an old friend – an expert like me can pick it out immediately. Now go home, and take that Gypsy with you. A painting doesn't have to be worth money to be valuable.'

Away he went into a far corner of his shop, leaving Danny to shove Gypsy into the carrier bag any old way, as if he was ashamed of her now that she was just plain cheap, and angry with her for making a fool out of him.

I hate that man! he thought as he crossed the road at Bedford Street lights, I hate him and his stupid shop and I hate his stupid carpets on his stupid walls.

How Will You Spend Gypsy? The game was over. Perhaps his mother had known all along. And Dr Moore. His Daddy, too. Maybe I was the only one who believed in Gypsy, thought Danny. The whole business filled him with such a deep, vague sadness that he wanted to be very, very young again.

When he got home his mother said, 'And where have you been to, my lad! And just be careful what you say because I think I know.'

'Mummy I just took it into that shop.'

'Did you! Well you had no business taking it anywhere, give it to me, here.'

She examined the picture carefully for signs of damage, and seemed satisfied.

'And what did they say in that shop?'

'I didn't go in,' Danny said quickly. 'I hadn't the nerve. Well, it was a big shop.'

All of a sudden his mother giggled, and gave him a peck on the cheek.

'Ah dear love you, sure you're only young.'

She fitted the picture over the lighter patch of wallpaper that marked the spot, and said, 'There you are now, Gypsy,' as if things were more or less back to normal.

Traffic Jam
FRANK MURPHY

Dermot did not remember when trains ran on the line near his home. The rails had been taken away and there was only a wide grassy path where he went for a walk every day with his dog, Razor. Sometimes he sat on the bridge over the road and watched the roofs of cars, vans, and lorries disappear under his feet.

He was there one day, counting the vehicles which passed by. A loud rumble came from round the bend of the road, and a few moments later a monster yellow lorry came into view. It came slowly on. Dermot had never seen one as big. It slowed down and came to a halt just before the bridge. Dermot could imagine the driver looking at the sign which said, 'Vehicles under 15 feet only'. He must have been satisfied because the lorry moved on slowly.

The boy saw the bonnet vanish under his feet, then the cab, and finally the box-like body of the lorry went slowly into the eye of the bridge. Then there was a frightening, grating sound of metal tearing against stone. The top of the lorry shivered and then the engine was switched off.

Razor barked in wild excitement and scuttled down the grass slope beside the bridge. Dermot followed at once. He went into the half dark under the bridge. The driver's head was out the window as he examined the roof of the lorry, jammed tight against the arch of the bridge. He muttered something under his breath and drew his head back inside the cab.

The engine started again. There was a whine as the back wheels of the lorry spun around at great speed, but the lorry did not move. Again and again the driver tried to back the lorry out of the bridge, but he failed each time. He got out and stood looking up at the top of the lorry, where it was jammed hard against the arch of the bridge. He moved to the other side, looked up again and scratched his head. He was puzzled.

Dermot spoke to him: 'Sir, I know –'

'Ah, run away out of that, Sonny, and don't be bothering me,' said the driver crossly.

'But, Sir –,' Dermot began again.

'Go away! I tell you,' growled the driver, and he sounded so angry that Dermot let him be.

Just then a horn sounded impatiently. A large black car had pulled up behind the lorry, and the driver was pressing on the horn. The lorry driver walked back to him.

'What's wrong?' asked the car driver.

'The lorry is stuck. I can't take it in or out,' answered the lorry driver. The car driver got out, and he and the lorry driver went forward and stood looking up at the arch. The car driver looked so knowing that Dermot thought he must be an expert on cars stuck in bridges. He thought he heard him say that something 'must be removed. There is no other way.'

Other cars arrived and stopped, until a line of cars, lorries, and vans stretched from the bridge down the road and round the bend. Drivers and passengers got out and came to the bridge. It was a narrow bridge and the lorry was stuck at the centre. No car could pass through.

After about ten minutes a large crowd had gathered. Most of the people just stood and looked, but five or six of them were speaking to the driver.

'The stones must be removed,' said a tall dark man in a light raincoat.

'Nonsense,' said a red-faced farmer in a floppy hat. 'If you take away the stones of the arch, the whole bridge will fall down.'

'The man is right,' said a young man with fair hair. 'There is only one way of getting it out. We must lower the roof of the lorry. Send for a sledge-hammer and we'll batter it down.'

''Tis hard to know which of you is the silliest,' said a van driver in a cloth cap. 'How could you get at the part of the roof that's stuck? Isn't it under the bridge?'

'Then what would *you* do?' asked a lady in a fur coat.

'Me?' said the van driver.

'Yes, you!'

'There's only one way,' said the van driver. 'Dig a hole in the road behind the wheels and lower the lorry that way.'

'I know a better way,' shouted Dermot.

'The hole might work,' said the farmer.

'I know a better way,' shouted Dermot again.

'I thought I told you to go home, Sonny,' said the lorry driver.

'Let the boy speak,' said the woman in the fur coat. 'His way couldn't be more stupid than some of yours. Speak up, boy!'

The people listened impatiently, because nobody expected

Dermot to have a good idea. 'Come on, boy. What have you to say?' said the van driver in the cloth cap.

'Let some of the air out of the wheels,' said Dermot simply.

'What?' asked the lorry driver in surprise.

'Let some of the air out of the wheels,' Dermot repeated.

'Ha-ha-ha haa,' laughed the farmer. 'The boy is right. His way is the answer.'

The lorry driver rushed to one of the front wheels and knelt down. The people heard a loud hiss. He did the same at all the other wheels. They looked up. The roof of the lorry was no longer jammed against the arch of the bridge. The engine was started, and the huge yellow monster moved forward slowly on soft wheels. It passed out the other side and the crowd cheered.

Later Dermot sat on the bridge, watching the long line of traffic pass under his feet. He was happy because there was a fifty-pence piece in his pocket, given to him by the lorry driver.

Sammy Gorman and the Light

JOAN LINGARD

Sammy Gorman was not the kind of man you'd automatically think of in terms of light. He was small and greyish, all over, from the top of his egg-shaped balding head down his fiddle-shaped face and bristly chin to the ancient suit which hung on him like on a coat hanger and the shoes which had once been black but now seemed to have no colour at all. But he talked about light.

'Have you seen the light?' he would ask, plucking your sleeve when he got close enough. I tried not to let him get too close but sometimes it would happen, when he was behind me in the bus queue or at the butcher's. Sometimes, too, he would offer me one of the peppermints that he sucked and I, not liking to refuse, would take one and put it in my mouth where I'd let it lie on the tip of my tongue, ready to be spat out the minute I left the shop.

'I'm very fond of a mint,' he would say, moving his from one side of his mouth to the other and letting me have a look at it and his greyish tongue in the process.

They were extra strong, the peppermints, and they almost took the tongue off you. At least they drowned out any other taste that they might have carried with them from the depths of his pockets, which also housed bits of string and elastic bands and snotty hankies and a small bible with print so small he had to hold it right up to his eyes. Though he seemed to know it all off by heart. 'Repent ye: for the kingdom of heaven is at hand. Though your sins be as scarlet, they shall be as white as snow.' It was always to do with sin and wickedness and repentance.

If I was with my friend Annie then we'd rush round the corner and nearly kill ourselves laughing. We'd end up collapsed against the wall, with stitches in our sides. But when I was on my own I'd slide away from him with my face all heated up and I'd lean over and spit the bitter little white sweet hard into the gutter. If you could believe Sammy Gorman the very gutters of Belfast were awash with sin.

Our family were church-goers but we weren't religious in the way that he was. I went to Sunday School and sang about Jesus loving me and the Green Hill that was far away, but apart from the first half-hour in school every morning when most of the kids tried to learn their spellings under the desk-lid while the teacher went on about Moses and the bulrushes or Cain and Abel, I didn't think much about it. Sammy, though, seemed to think about nothing else.

He didn't go to a proper church, with a spire and an organ and stained-glass windows; he went to a hall at the top of the road. They didn't believe in music or coloured glass or any of that nonsense. And they didn't smoke, or drink alcohol or take stimulants of any kind. That meant tea and coffee too. Killjoys, my father called them.

'No one has to drink if they don't want to,' said my mother. 'Sometimes drink can kill things too.' She spoke rather sharply, for her. She also said that everyone was entitled to his own persuasion.

The trouble was that Sammy wanted to persuade everyone else to join his. For, of course, when he asked you if you'd seen the light he meant, Had you seen *his* light? When I was little I'd thought he'd meant something to do with showing a light at the window for the war was on then and we had to be terribly careful about the black-out in case anyone thought we were signalling to the Jerries.

He was a damned nuisance, was Sammy Gorman, said my father. He was harmless, said my mother, who would listen politely while he read aloud to her in the street from the Book of Ezekiel.

It must be perfectly obvious that Sammy, from the account I've given of his clothes, had no wife. But he did have a sister. Mrs McIlwrath was a widow woman, with one daughter, Violet, who was the same age as me. Annie and I called her Smellie. My mother said we were horrible little girls.

They lived in the house opposite us, Violet, her mother and her Uncle Sammy. The house was spotless, even though Sammy was not, and you could eat off the floor, so Mrs McIlwrath was fond of saying, though none of us had ever seen inside to find out and the front windows were smothered in thick net. It was not the kind of house (like ours) where people came and went at all hours of the day and night and drank cups of coffee or mugs of beer or sat in at the table if it happened to be a mealtime. Mrs McIlwrath liked to keep herself to herself, so she said. She held her nose tilted upwards when she said it.

'Not a woman I could ever take to,' said my father, sliding his arm round my mother's waist.

'It can't be easy having Sammy living with her, but,' said my mother and no doubt it was not, for to have him sitting at your dinner table would be a sore trial. They were all of the same religious persuasion, however, so I supposed they wouldn't mind him reading aloud to them about sin while they ate.

'Youse two'll not go to heaven,' said Violet to Annie and me. 'You've not seen the light.'

'You're off your rocker so you are,' said Annie. 'And where do you think we'll go then?' she asked, tempting Violet to say the word out loud.

Violet, her round glasses glinting, came up close and breathed the letters in our faces. All four of them.

'You swore so you did, Smellie McIlwrath!' I cried.

'I'm telling!' said Annie. 'Smellie McIlwrath swore! It's you that'll go *there*.'

Annie and I did a little jig around Violet screeching, 'Smellie McIlwrath said a swear word! Smellie McIlwrath swore! She's going to go to you know where!'

She went home with tears running down inside of her round shiny glasses and Annie and I did our falling about and killing ourselves laughing act again. It didn't take much to set us off.

The next time I saw Violet she said, 'There's one thing for sure – your father'll not go to heaven. My mother said so.' And she tilted her nose up the way her mother did.

'What does she know about it?'

'She saw him coming home last night – drunk! He's a drunkard.'

'He is not!'

'He is sot!'

'You're a liar!'

'I am not! My mother saw him, my mother saw –'

I biffed her one on the nose then and sent the shiny round glasses flying. The frames lay on the ground, both lenses shattered. Blood streamed from Violet's nose. She set up a howl and I ran home and hid in the garden shed where I stayed until my eldest brother came to fetch me.

'You'd better come,' he said. 'The Wrath is on the warpath and our mother's facing the music.'

Mrs McIlwrath was standing on our front step – she would never accept invitations to come in, thinking perhaps she might be corrupted – dangling Violet's broken glasses about an inch from my mother's face.

'Did you do this, Ruth?' asked my mother. 'Did you hit Violet on the face?'

I nodded.

'What have you to say for yourself?'

What could I say? That I was defending my father against a charge of being a drunk? He's not a drunk, he's not, I told myself fiercely, as I stood there watching the bent frames of the spectacles swing to and fro. He was fond of a drink, that was all, and liked to have a bit of a crack with his pals in the pub. He always came home in a good mood from the pub, usually brought us chips from the chip shop, and sometimes a fish for my mother. 'Buying me off are you?' she'd say and he'd say, 'Ah, come on, Maureen my love . . .' But I didn't want to think about that now. I felt as if I was about to topple over from watching the frames moving backwards and forwards, backwards and forwards.

'You'd better go inside, Ruth,' said my mother, breaking my trance.

'I know what I'd do with her if she was mine,' I heard Mrs McIlwrath say as I climbed the stairs.

'We shall pay for Violet's glasses to be repaired,' said my mother. 'And I'm sorry for any inconvenience that Violet will be caused.'

Violet came to school without her homework done the next day. She had a note with her. The teacher read it and then shook her head at me and Violet smiled. She could see anything she wanted to see.

'Baby, baby!' we chanted at her in the playground. 'Tell-tale tit! Your mouth is full of –!'

On the way home from school that afternoon we stopped at the air-raid shelter round the corner from our street. The war was over, the streetlights had been switched on long ago, but no one had yet come to take down the air-raid shelters. They'd never been used, not for sheltering from raids anyway, people had preferred to stay in their own houses and get under the table or the stairs – they were made of brick and smelt musty and damp – though from time to time tramps hung out in them, or courting couples. They wouldn't be very romantic places to court in, Annie and I agreed. We'd once or twice dared one another to go inside but had only ever taken a quick look in and run out again. Our parents had forbidden us to go in; they said you never knew who might be there.

Annie took a stick of blue chalk from her pocket and wrote in large letters on the side of the shelter: Smellie McIlwrath is a Tell-Tale Tit. I kept watch while she did it. She passed the chalk to me and I wrote: And Her Mouth Is Full Of –. We then put the chalk down the nearest drain – to hide the evidence – and cleaned our hands on the insides of our skirts.

Putting on our most innocent of looks, we strolled on. As we passed the entrance of the air-raid shelter I glanced in and saw – of all things – a light!

'Annie, I've seen the light!'

'What? What light?'

I dragged her back to the doorway of the shelter. There was no door and never had been. 'I saw one,' I whispered. 'Inside.'

Her eyes widened.

'Maybe it was a ghost?' I suggested.

She said I was bonkers so I dared her to have a look. 'We'll both look,' I said.

We joined hands and took one step inside and sure enough, there was the light, in the far corner. We blinked and in that second it went out. We fled.

But although the light had been on for only a second I had had time to see the two eyes shining above it.

'It was Sammy Gorman,' I said, when we'd reached the corner and recovered our breath.

'It couldn't have been,' said Annie.

'It was.'

Was that what he meant by seeing the light? Had it nothing to do with religion after all?

All next day in school I kept thinking about it. Violet was absent. Sick, said the teacher, who had received another note from Mrs McIlwrath. When the bell rang at the end of the afternoon the teacher called to Annie and me to stay back.

'Are you bullying Violet McIlwrath?' she asked. 'Her mother says you are.'

'No, miss,' we chorused.

'I hope you're not.'

She let us go.

As we walked across the playground I said, 'I'm going to take a look inside the shelter. I've got a torch with me.'

'What if it's *not* Sammy Gorman?' said Annie and shivered. 'What if it's a maniac?'

We could run, I said. But what if it was Sammy Gorman? What would we say to him? Hello, Sammy, are you seeing the light?

We slowed our steps as we neared the shelter. The street was empty, the kids would have run home from school and be changing into their playing clothes before going out again. We looked to right and left and then went straight to the entrance. The smell of mustiness filled our noses and Annie let out a short sneeze before she could hold it back.

The shelter was black as pitch inside. I clicked on my torch and sent the small beam into the space. There was no one there. No one at all. I fanned the light over the floor and the walls and even the ceiling.

'What's that?' said Annie, pointing to one of the far corners.

It looked like an old sack. Our hearts pounded. Should we go right in? We hadn't counted on doing that. We clutched one another and tiptoed over to the corner. The smells became heavier, a mixture of mould and urine and cat. I swallowed, to stop myself from throwing up. I couldn't understand how anyone, not even a tramp, would want to spend two minutes in the place.

We were at the corner now. We bent down and together lifted the sack. Something glinted on the patch of floor which we'd uncovered.

'It's a bottle,' said Annie.

I picked it up and we saw that it was half full of golden liquid. In the light of the torch we examined the label. Bushmills Irish whiskey, it said.

'Whiskey!' gasped Annie.

'Sammy must have been drinking it!'

We heard footsteps outside. We froze like in a game of statues. The feet passed by.

'Let's get out of here!' said Annie.

Quickly, I replaced the bottle and the sack and we scuttled back towards the light of the doorway. Outside, the brightness surprised us. Our hands were streaked with dirt. We wanted to laugh but couldn't quite manage it. Only the odd giggle and gulp came out of us. We went home to Annie's house to get cleaned up.

'That must be why Sammy's always sucking peppermints,' I said. 'To kill the smell of the whiskey.'

'Wait till we tell this to Miss Smellie Boots!' I didn't answer so Annie said, 'What's up with you? What are you screwing your face up for?'

I shrugged. 'I was just thinking that maybe we shouldn't tell on Sammy.'

'Why not?'

'Well, he's not done us any harm. And just think –'

We pondered on the trouble he'd get into with his sister. It seemed to me it wouldn't be fair to wish that on anybody.

'Maybe you're right,' said Annie reluctantly. 'It's a pity all the same.'

I nodded.

The funny thing was though that the next time Violet tried to get a rise out of me by telling me that my father was a drunkard, I just walked straight past and wasn't even tempted to say, 'What about your uncle?' I knew more than she did. I had a secret. I looked back at her and smiled.

And Sammy Gorman never did ask me again if I'd seen the light.

Last Bus for Christmas
PATRICIA LYNCH

'Hurry up there, Miheal! Will ye bring over two red candles quick!'

'More strawberry jam, Miheal! Two one-pound jars! And raisins: four one-pound bags!'

'Miheal Daly! I'm wore out wid waitin' for twine. How can I parcel the customers' groceries wid ne'er an inch of string?'

Miheal grabbed a handful of string from the box in the corner behind the biscuit tins and ran with it to Mr Coughlan. He brought the jam and the raisins at the same time to Peter Cadogan, and rolled the candles along the counter to Jim Reardon. Then he went back to his job of filling half-pound bags with sugar.

Miheal was the shop-boy and, one day, if he worked hard and behaved himself, Mr Coughlan had promised to make him an assistant.

'There's grandeur for an orphan!' Mrs Coughlan told him. 'Ye should be grateful.'

Miheal was grateful. But, as he watched the women crowding the other side of the counter, filling market bags and baskets with Christmas shopping, he was discontented. Yet he had whistled and sung as he put up the coloured paper chains and decorated the window with yards of tinsel and artificial holly.

He nibbled a raisin and gazed out at the sleet drifting past the open door.

Everybody's going home for Christmas but me, he thought.

The Coughlans always went to their relations for Christmas. Mrs Coughlan left Miheal plenty to eat and Mr Coughlan gave him a shilling to spend. But Miheal never ate his Christmas dinner until they came back. After Mass he spent Christmas Day walking about the streets, listening to the noise and clatter that came from the houses.

'Only two more hours,' whispered Peter Cadogan, as Miheal brought him bags of biscuits and half-pounds of rashers as fast as Mr Coughlan could cut them.

'Two more sugars, Miheal,' said Jim Reardon. 'Where d'you get your bus?'

Jim was new. He didn't know Miheal was an orphan, and Miheal was ashamed to tell him he had no home to go to for Christmas.

'Aston's Quay,' he muttered.

'We'll go together,' said Jim over his shoulder. 'I've me bag under the counter. Get yours!'

The next time Miheal brought Jim candles and raisins the new assistant wanted to know what time Miheal's bus went.

'I'll just make it if I run,' said Miheal.

'Then get yer bag, lad. Get yer bag!'

Miheal slipped through the door leading to the house. He ran to his little dark room under the stairs. He didn't dare switch on the light. Mrs Coughlan would want to know what he was doing. And a nice fool he'd look if she found out he was pretending to go home for Christmas.

'Home!' said Miheal to himself. 'That's where a lad's people come from and mine came from Carrigasheen.'

He wrapped his few belongings in an old waterproof. He grabbed his overcoat from the hook behind the door and was back in the shop before Mr Coughlan could miss him.

'Hi, Miheal! Give me a hand with this side of bacon. I never cut so many rashers in me life!'

Miheal pushed his bundle under the counter and ran to help.

'Isn't it grand to be going home for Christmas!' cried Peter, as they closed the door to prevent any more customers from coming in.

'Isn't it terrible to be turning money away!' groaned Mr Coughlan.

But Mrs Coughlan was waiting for him in her best hat and the coat with the fur collar.

'Can I trust you lads to bolt the shop door an' let yerselves out be the side door?' demanded Mr Coughlan.

'Indeed you can, sir!' replied Peter and Jim.

The last customer was served.

'I'm off!' cried Peter.

'Safe home!' called the others.

Then Jim was running down the quay, Miheal stumbling after him, clasping his bundle, his unbuttoned coat flapping in the wind.

They went along Burgh Quay, pushing by the people waiting for the Bray bus, then across to Aston's Quay.

'There's me bus!' shouted Jim.

''Tis packed full!' murmured Miheal. He was terribly sorry for Jim. But maybe he'd come back with him and they could spend Christmas together.

The bus was moving.

Jim gave a leap, the conductor caught his arm and pulled him to safety. He turned and waved to Miheal, his round red face laughing. He would have to stand all the way, but Jim was used to standing.

54

Two queues still waited. Miheal joined the longest.

'Where are ye bound for, avic?' asked a stout country-woman, with a thin little girl and four large bundles, who came up after him.

'Carrigasheen!' replied Miheal proudly.

'Ah, well! I never heard tell of the place. But no doubt ye'll be welcome when ye get there. An' here's the bus.'

'I'll help with the bundles, ma'am,' said Miheal politely.

Now every seat was filled. Still more people squeezed into the bus. Miheal reached the step.

'One more, an' one more only!' announced the conductor. 'In ye go, ma'am!' said Miheal, stepping back.

The little girl was in. Miheal pushed the bundles after her and everyone cried out when the conductor tried to keep back the stout woman.

'Sure ye can't take the child away from her mammy!' declared a thin man. 'Haven't ye any Christianity in yer bones?'

'Can't she sit on me lap?' demanded the stout woman. 'Give me a h'ist up, lad. And God reward ye!' she added, turning to Miheal.

He seized her under the arms. She caught the shining rail and Miheal gave a great heave.

He stood gazing after the bus.

'Now I'm stranded!' he said, forgetting he had no need to leave Dublin.

A dash of sleet in Miheal's face reminded him. He could go back to the lonely house behind the shop. His supper would be waiting on the table in the kitchen. He could poke up the fire and read his library book.

The quays were deserted. A tall garda strolled along. He stared curiously at Miheal and his bundle.

'Missed the bus, lad?' he asked.

''Twas full up,' explained Miheal.

'Bad luck!' sympathized the garda. 'Can ye go back where ye came from?'

Miheal nodded.

' 'Tis a bad night to be travelling!' said the garda. 'That's the way to look at it.'

He gave Miheal a friendly nod and passed on.

I'd as well be getting me supper, thought Miheal.

But he did not move.

Over the Metal Bridge came a queer old coach drawn by two horses. The driver was wrapped in a huge coat with many capes and a broad-brimmed hat was pulled down over his twinkling eyes.

He flourished a whip and pulled up beside Miheal.

The boy edged away. He didn't like the look of the coach at all.

The driver leaned over and managed to open the door at the back with his whip.

'In ye get! Last bus for Christmas!'

Whoever saw a bus with horses! thought Miheal. But I suppose they use any old traps at Christmas.

Still he held back.

'All the way to Carrigasheen widout stoppin'!' said the driver.

Miheal could see the cushioned seats and the floor spread thick with fresh hay. The wind, which was growing fiercer and colder every moment, blew in his face. He gave one look along the desolate quay and, putting his foot on the iron step, scrambled in.

At once the door slammed shut. The driver gave a shout and the horses trotted over the stones.

The coach bumped and swayed. Miheal tried to stretch out on the seat, but he slipped to the floor. The hay was thick and clean. He put his bundle under his head for a pillow and fell asleep.

An extra bump woke him up.

'I never thought to ask the fare,' said Miheal to himself. 'Seems a long way, so it does. Would he want ten shillings? He might – easy! Well, I haven't ten shillings. I've two new half-crowns. He'll get one and not a penny more!'

He tried to stand up, but the coach was swaying from side to side and he had to sit down again.

'Mister! Mister!' he shouted. 'How much is the fare?'

The rattling of the coach and the thunder of the horses' hooves made so much noise he could scarcely hear himself. Yet he would not keep quiet.

'I won't pay a penny more than two and six,' he shouted. 'Mind now! I'm telling you.'

The door of the coach swung open and Miheal was pitched out, his bundle following him. He landed on a bank covered with snow and lay there blinking.

The road wound away through the mountains in the moonlight – an empty desolate road. The wind had dropped but snow was falling.

In the distance he could hear a strange sound. It was coming nearer and nearer, and soon Miheal knew it was someone singing '*Adeste Fideles*' in a queer cracked voice.

The singer approached, tramping slowly along: an old man with a heavy sack on his back.

'What ails ye to be sitting there in the snow, at this late hour of the night, young lad?' he asked, letting his sack slip to the ground.

'I came on the coach from Dublin,' replied Miheal, standing up.

He was ashamed to say he had fallen out.

The old man pushed back his battered caubeen and scratched his head.

'But there hasn't been a coach on this road in mortal memory!' he declared. 'There's the bus road the other side of the mountain and the last bus went by nigh on two hours ago. I suppose ye came by that. Where are ye bound for?'

'Mebbe I did come by the bus and mebbe I didn't!' exclaimed Miheal. 'But I'd be thankful if you'd tell me am I right for Carrigasheen?'

The old man wasn't a bit annoyed by Miheal's crossness.

'D'ye see the clump of trees where the road bends round by

the mountain? There's Carrigasheen! I'm on me way there an' I'll be real glad of company. So ye're home for Christmas? I thought I knew everyone for miles around, yet I don't remember yer face. What name is on ye, lad?'

'Miheal Daly.'

The old man stared.

'There are no Dalys in Carrigasheen now. That I do know! But we can talk as we go. Me own name is Paudeen Caffrey.'

Miheal caught up the sack. He was a strong lad but he found it heavy. He wondered how the old man had managed to carry it at all. Paudeen Caffrey took the boy's bundle and they set off. The snow piled on their shoulders, on the loads they carried, on their hair, their eyebrows, but they did not notice, for Miheal was telling the old man all about himself.

'So me poor gossoon, ye're an orphan,' asked the old man.

'I am indeed!' agreed Miheal.

'An' ye haven't a father or mother, or brother or sister to be a friend to ye?'

'Not a soul!'

'An' these people ye work for, what class of people are they?' continued old Paudeen Caffrey.

'Not too bad!' declared Miheal. 'Aren't they going to make me an assistant one of these days?'

'Suppose now,' began the old man. 'Mind, I'm just saying suppose – ye have a chance to be shop-boy to an old man and his wife that needed help bad in their shop and couldn't get it? Mind ye – I'm only supposing. Ye'd have a room wid two windas, one lookin' out on the market square, the other at the mountains. Ye'd have three good meals a day, a snack at supper, ten shillings a week, an' if ye wanted to keep a dog or a cat, or a bicycle, ye'd be welcome. What would ye say to that?'

He looked at Miheal sideways and Miheal looked back.

'It wouldn't be with Paudeen Caffrey, that kept the corner shop next the post office, would it?' asked Miheal.

'It would so,' replied the old man.

'I'm remembering now,' said the boy. 'Me father told me if ever I needed a friend to write to Paudeen Caffrey.'

'Why didn't ye, lad? Why didn't ye?'

'I was ashamed. Me mother told me how they left Carri-gasheen after telling everyone they were going to Dublin to make their fortunes an', when they came back, they'd be riding in their carriage. Ye see?'

The old man laughed.

'An' didn't ye come back in a carriage? But there's the lights of Carrigasheen. Do ye come home wid me, Miheal Daly?'

'If you'll have me, Mr Caffrey.'

'The old man chuckled.

'An' to think I went out for a sack of praties an' come back wid a shop-boy! Wasn't it well ye caught the last bus for Christ-mas, Miheal?'

'It was indeed!' declared Miheal Daly.

He could see the corner shop with the door open and an old woman looking out. Beyond her he caught a glimpse of fire-light dancing on the walls, of holy pictures framed in holly and a big red Christmas candle on the table waiting for the youngest in the house to light it.

The Sunflowers in the Snow

WILLIAM TREVOR

Once upon a time a really fantastic thing happened. In a town in Ireland some sunflowers bloomed in December.

It was a few days before Christmas and there were four inches of snow on the ground. 'The sunflowers imagine it's August,' said the people of the town. They didn't know what to think.

'Well?' said Dom, a red-haired boy, to Mr Cranley, the butcher.

'I haven't seen them yet,' said Mr Cranley. 'I'll go up one of these days.'

Dom wondered about that. He wondered about Mr Cranley, for he knew that Mr Cranley must know more than most people about the sunflowers. Mr Cranley placed his two hands on his butcher's block and looked down at Dom. He said:

'You can't understand everything, Dom. It would be a dull old world if you could.'

Mr Cranley was the only person in the small town that Dom had ever told his favourite secret to. One day, a year or so ago, he had explained to Mr Cranley about how he used to look out of his bedroom window, watching the people and the seagulls.

Sometimes Mr McCarthy the ironmonger would pass by, taking his dog Bonzo for a walk on a lead, and when that happened Dom would quickly close his eyes and see everything differently. What he saw was Bonzo taking Mr McCarthy for a walk on a lead, and this always made Dom laugh and laugh.

Sometimes when he looked across the street and saw old Mrs Twing feeding the sparrows on her window-sill, Dom would close his eyes and see the sparrows feeding old Mrs Twing. And when Danny Fowler, the milkman, drove up the street with his horse and cart Dom would close his eyes and see Danny Fowler dragging the cart, while Trot, the horse delivered the milk bottles. That made Dom laugh so much that his mother would shout up to him to stop at once or there'd be trouble. His mother used to say it was his red hair that made him so excitable.

When Dom told Mr Cranley all that, Mr Cranley said: 'You have a Special Gift, Dom. Like someone might have a Special Gift and be able to play beautiful music on a piano or a violin. Or be able to run faster than anyone else. Nobody understands why some people can do things and other people can't.'

'Have you a Special Gift, Mr Cranley?' Dom asked.

Mr Cranley didn't reply to that question.

He was a large, sad man with an extremely red face, who

was very honest and always told the truth. He was always getting angry in the presence of his customers. He would strike his butcher's block with his chopper and complain about the meat that was being produced these days. 'Look at this horrible liver,' Mr Cranley would cry. 'And those revolting kidneys. Meat isn't what it used to be.'

Now, of course the more Mr Cranley made such remarks about his own meat the more the people of the town refused to buy it, until in the end nobody came to Mr Cranley's shop at all. They used to have to get on to a bus and go to another butcher in a town four miles away, which is a long way to have to go for a piece of meat.

From his bedroom window or when he was out and about Dom had watched most of the people in the town, and he had come to the conclusion that Mr Cranley was by far the most interesting.

For one thing, Mr Cranley was always alone. He never went out with a dog or a horse so that Dom could change the two about like he did with Mr McCarthy and Danny Fowler. Once he watched Mr Cranley chopping up some bones, and he closed his eyes and tried to imagine that the bones were chopping up Mr Cranley, but it didn't work. He hadn't expected it to work, because he had guessed that Mr Cranley wasn't like other people. He began to watch Mr Cranley very closely indeed. He always followed him when he went for walks.

The day after the sunflowers bloomed in the snow, Mr Cranley put on his big black overcoat and walked to the edge of the town to see for himself. It was a particularly cold day and the cold got into Mr Cranley's ears and hurt them, making Mr Cranley sadder than ever. He said to himself that it was a sorry enough thing to be a butcher without customers but to be a butcher with painful ears instead was just about the limit.

While Mr Cranley was thinking this a bus passed him by

on the road, and the bus driver hooted his horn. Mr Cranley looked up and waved, but nobody waved back, because the bus was full of mothers and children on their way to the other town to buy meat for Christmas, and they didn't at all care for the sight of Mr Cranley idling by the roadside. A tear rolled from Mr Cranley's right eye, down his large red cheek, and dropped on to the snow.

Just then a car pulled up beside him and two important-looking men got out and marched towards the sunflowers.

Mr Cranley watched them. They poked at the flowers. They smelled them and felt their petals between their thumbs and forefingers. One of them scooped the snow away from the root of a plant and cut through the hard earth with a penknife to get a look at the root itself.

When they'd finished all that, the men walked back to the car very slowly. They were talking in quiet voices as they approached Mr Cranley, and Mr Cranley said:

'Good afternoon, gentlemen.'

'Yes,' said one of the men in a rather rude way, not paying much attention to Mr Cranley.

'I'm the local butcher,' explained Mr Cranley, thinking that the men might be impressed by that. He added because he couldn't help it: 'Meat isn't what it used to be.'

'Yes,' said the same man, in the same way, and whispered something to his friend. They seemed amused by the sight of Mr Cranley with his red face and his big black overcoat.

'What do you think of those sunflowers?' said Mr Cranley. 'Is it a miracle?'

The men laughed. Miracles, they informed Mr Cranley, were a thing of the past. One laughed more loudly than the other. 'You'll be telling us the fairies planted them next,' he said.

Mr Cranley laughed too. 'No, no,' he said. 'We're very modern here, you know. We don't at all believe in fairies.'

Now, during all this time – from the first moment that Mr Cranley had stopped by the sunflowers and felt the pain in his ears – Dom had been hiding behind a tree. He had seen the busload of mothers and children go by, he had seen Mr Cranley wave at them, he had seen the tear on Mr Cranley's cheek, he had seen the car stop and the two important-looking men get out. He could hear what they were saying and what Mr Cranley was saying, and he was very interested because he had his own idea about why the sunflowers had bloomed in December.

'There is a scientific explanation for those sunflowers,' Dom heard one of the men say. 'They can't just come there at the wrong time of year.'

'You'd think the cold would kill them,' remarked Mr Cranley.

The men laughed. 'That's just the point,' they said.

Dom watched the men climb into their car and drive away. He watched Mr Cranley stand for a while by the roadside looking after the car. Dom imagined that Mr Cranley was thinking that the men might at least have offered him a lift back to his shop. He watched the butcher heave a big sigh and set off on his own along the snowy road.

Dom knew that Mr Cranley knew something about the sunflowers because one day, a few months ago, he had seen Mr Cranley planting the seeds.

Dom slipped from behind the tree and followed Mr Cranley along the road. He walked slowly, taking care to be ready to dart away if Mr Cranley should look round, because he knew that Mr Cranley wouldn't care to find himself being followed. But Mr Cranley didn't look round and Dom followed him all the way to his butcher's shop, where there was one old chop and a half-pound of sausages hanging in the window. Mr Cranley entered the shop and looked about him at all the emptiness. He looked through the window and saw Dom lurking outside.

'I've seen the sunflowers,' he shouted through the glass. 'I think they'll die after Christmas.'

Then he bolted the door and went upstairs.

Dom watched for a little while longer. He saw the light go on in Mr Cranley's bedroom and he guessed that although it was only half past three in the afternoon Mr Cranley would probably go to bed and read the newspaper because he couldn't think of anything else to do. It made Dom sad to think of poor Mr Cranley in bed with a newspaper, with no wife to talk to and no children to cheer him up. It made him sad when he thought that if Mr Cranley hadn't been so honest he would be a successful butcher instead of one whom nobody could be bothered with. 'Why ever did he plant the sunflower seeds?' said Dom to himself. 'What on earth sort of a strange man is this?'

The next day lots and lots of other important-looking men arrived in the town. They were scientists, and reporters from the newspapers, and people from the Television. The hotel, Kelly's Atlantic, was packed on every floor, and the fifteen public houses in the town had to take in some of the visitors.

The television cameras took pictures of the sunflowers so that everyone in the world could see what sunflowers in the December snow looked like, and all the scientists disagreed about why they were in bloom.

Mr Kelly of Kelly's Atlantic Hotel appeared on television in his striped blue suit. He said he couldn't understand the sunflowers standing up to the weather like that. He added, though, that it was good for business.

In the middle of that same night – it was the night before Christmas Eve – Mr Cranley disappeared. When the morning came, his butcher's shop didn't open and the only person who noticed this fact was Dom. He peeped through the window and could see nothing except the old chop and the half-pound of sausages. All Mr Cranley's choppers and knives and saws were gone and the butcher's block was scrubbed and dry.

'Mr Cranley has gone away,' said Dom to one of the

newspaper reporters. 'It was Mr Cranley who planted the sunflower seeds in August.'

'What's this, son?' said the newspaper reporter, taking a pipe out of his mouth.

The police came and opened up Mr Cranley's shop to see if Mr Cranley was still in bed maybe. They thought he might be ill, for although he was a bad butcher they were quite prepared to help him. But Mr Cranley was gone. His clothes were gone. His one suitcase was gone. 'So that's the end of Mr Cranley,' said the people of the town.

'What's this red-haired youngster saying?' asked all the scientists, having heard about Dom's story.

They all came round to Dom's house and Dom's mother made them cups of tea, and Dom told them why the sunflowers had bloomed in December.

'Mr Cranley had a Special Gift,' said Dom, 'which he wouldn't talk about. It's something you get given.'

The scientists sipped their hot tea and smiled.

'There must be a scientific reason for the sunflowers,' said the scientists. 'You can't get away from that.'

'I have a Special Gift,' said Dom. 'I can close my eyes and change things round.'

The scientists began to talk among themselves. 'So this funny old butcher put in sunflower seeds in August and they flowered in December,' they said. 'We're no closer to the truth than that.'

'We are! We are!' cried Dom. 'I know about Mr Cranley. I watched him. He's not like other people. He has –'

'A Special Gift,' said one of the scientists, and all the others laughed.

Dom became so angry then, jumping up and down and stamping his feet on the floor, that his mother had to tell him to stop or there'd be trouble. So he calmed down.

'Mr Cranley has gone away,' he said, 'to use his Special Gift somewhere else.'

The scientists nodded their heads. They didn't at all believe that Mr Cranley had a Special Gift.

66

'In the old days,' said Dom, 'wizards had a Special Gift. And witches. That was why people were afraid of them. Nobody knows why some people can do things and other people can't.'

'Look here, laddie,' said one of the scientists, 'no one could have a gift like you say Mr Cranley has.'

'Why not?' said Dom.

'Because never in the history of the world,' replied the scientist, 'has anyone been able to arrange for sunflowers to appear all of a sudden through four inches of snow.'

'That is because no one ever had that Special Gift before. You can't understand everything.'

The scientists smiled. 'We think we can,' they said quietly, 'if we try hard enough.'

'No, you can't,' cried Dom, jumping up and down again. 'Mr Cranley said you can't understand everything. He said it would be a dull old world if you could.'

'Now, now,' said the scientists.

'It's his red hair that makes him do it,' said Dom's mother, and she shook her head crossly at him when the scientists weren't looking.

'The flowers are there for Christmas,' said Dom. 'After Christmas they will die.'

The scientists all shook their heads. 'We don't know that, laddie,' the one who had called him laddie before said. 'We don't know that at all.'

'Well, I do,' said Dom.

'How do you know?' asked the scientists all together.

'Because Mr Cranley told me.'

On the day after Christmas Day the sunflowers wilted and died. The scientists were amazed.

'How did the old butcher know?' they said to one another.

They looked for Mr Cranley but they could not find him.

In the end they packed their suitcases and left the little town with everything about the sunflowers written down in their notebooks.

'Well?' said Dom, seeing them going off.

'Goodbye, Dom,' said the scientists.

'You can't understand everything,' said Dom. 'Now, can you?'

The scientists didn't reply. They looked at their watches and said the train was late.

'Well?' said Dom.

One of the scientists blew his nose. The others stared seriously at the ground.

'It would be a dull old world if you could,' said Dom.

The scientists didn't say anything.

The Decision
STELLA MAHON

'I don't care who they are!' Mrs Dougan was saying in her righteously indignant voice, and wearing a face to match. 'They've no right to stick things on my gable wall.'

'You'd better not let them'uns next door hear you gettin' on like that.' The warning came from her husband. He was joking, but Mrs Dougan was in no mood to take cracks about their neighbours' avid political partisanship.

'I don't care what they hear – it's my gable wall. People should ask you first,' she went on.

'I expect they just take it for granted that everybody's Unionist, and won't mind having posters all over the place. It's hard, right enough, to find anybody in this part of Belfast who isn't Unionist!'

'Whether I am or whether I'm not, it makes no difference. The cheek of it . . .'

She was interrupted in her railings by the noisy entrance of their seven-year-old daughter.

'Mind wer door will ye, Sheila?' The reprimand was delivered with a long suffering which indicated it as a frequent one. But Sheila paid no attention.

'Daddy, there are a whole lot of flags stuck on our wall. Who put them there? Did you put them there?'

'*No* he did not, well dare he,' called Mrs Dougan from the scullery, where she was brewing tea to help her frayed nerves.

'No I didn't,' said Mr Dougan, though much more calmly.

'Well, who did? What're they for?' Sheila wanted to know.

'They're for the election,' her father replied.

'What's that?'

Mrs Dougan pre-empted her husband's reply. 'Now just you never mind talking politics to thon child. There's enough politics in this house without you rearing her to think of them.' Mr Dougan was a member of the Communist Party. Mrs Dougan did not approve, and it was one of those things, if ever mentioned at all, which was talked about in the hushed tones usually reserved for referring to a terminal illness.

'It's not politics to tell her what a general election is,' protested Mr Dougan.

'It is when you get started,' retorted his wife.

Mr Dougan ignored all this, and began to explain the mechanics of elections in very simple terms to his daughter: how people were picked to go and work in Parliament to decide things about running the country. He was sure Sheila was capable of grasping the basics. She was fairly smart for her age.

'Well, why has the election stuck flags all over our wall?' she asked, in a pause during her father's lecture on elementary politics.

'Ach, Sheila,' he sounded impatient. 'The election is for picking the people. The people who want to get picked want to tell everyone their names, so they put posters on the walls.'

'That's enough now,' Mrs Dougan intervened.

'She has to know these things!'

'Not when she's only seven, she doesn't,' snapped Sheila's mother. 'Elections are for big people, not wee girls,' she said to her daughter, with an air of finality which was well known to the child, and signalled clearly that enough was indeed enough. Sheila got up and went outside to have another look at the posters.

Across the middle of the Union Jack printed on each poster there was some writing. 'This we will . . .' read Sheila, and stopped. The next word was a big one, and good reader though she was, it had her stumped. She mulled the letters over in her mind. It looked like 'mountain' – but only at the end. The first half of it looked nearly like the second half. So it should sound the same in both bits. Well, she knew how to say the end bit, from knowing 'mountain'. So, via this circuitous route, she deduced that the mystery word was 'menten'. She read it out loud for effect. 'This we will menten.' It didn't make any sense. Choosing to risk her mother's displeasure, she went into the house to ask her father about it.

'Daddy, the flags say "This we will menten". What does that mean?'

'What?' asked her father.

'"This we will menten," they say,' quoted Sheila again.

Her father laughed. Even Mrs Dougan couldn't help a smile.

'Oh, no, they say "maintain".'

'Oh, "maintain",' repeated Sheila. She ran out to have another look. Knowing the right way to say the word had a magic all of its own which blotted out the fact that she still didn't know what it meant.

She was reading the slogan off each poster as her friend Margaret came skipping along the street.

'I know what that says,' announced Sheila proudly, and demonstrated her skill.

'Ya, smarty Alec! D'ye want to skip?' was Margaret's snappy but good-natured reply.

'Aye, all right,' said Sheila, not too enthusiastically. She didn't much care for skipping two to a rope. They jumped together, Margaret turning.

'My daddy says the flags are there for the election,' Sheila announced.

'Eleven – I know – twelve,' replied her friend as she counted. 'Ach, look where yer jumpin'.' Sheila had mistimed herself and caught the rope under her foot. 'We only got to twelve.' Margaret was quite cross.

They were just getting ready to begin again, when a large car came round the corner. It had a loudspeaker on the top. The girls listened.

'. . . here tonight at seven. Come out and hear him. Don't forget, your Unionist candidate for the Fifties, here tonight at seven. Vote Unionist!'

The message was repeated over and over again as the car moved along the street, and disappeared round the corner into the next one. The two friends discussed the import of the message. Sheila was really quite excited. It was all so new, and at tea time she was full of it.

'Did yous hear the car that came round?' she asked.

Her father said he had. Her mother bewailed the fact that they obviously were not even going to be allowed to eat in peace without more election talk.

'What was it about?' asked Sheila's brother Sammy, who had missed the event.

'It was about the election,' Sheila came in quickly, eager to demonstrate her grasp of the new word.

'I wasn't asking you, smarty. I was asking m'Da.'

'Ach, it was just about yer man from the Unionist Party. Coming round the streets tonight to give the usual speeches to the populace.'

'I'm going to the pictures, I'll miss him,' said Sammy.

'Miss what?' asked Mr Dougan sarcastically.

He and his son laughed. Mrs Dougan tut-tutted and said that elections brought out the bad side of people.

'No bad side at all. Sure it's always the same old stuff.'

'Billy, less of that now. You'll get your say when you put thon wee "X" on the ballot paper.'

'What say?' her husband remarked. He was full of sarcasm tonight all right.

'All the say anybody has,' his wife reminded him.

Sheila re-entered the conversation by asking her father whom he would be voting for. He said he would probably vote for the Labour man. She directed the same question at her mother, who announced that she very likely wouldn't bother her head going near a polling station.

'Ach, c'mon now,' said Mr Dougan. 'You always vote and you say you won't every year. But you always go.'

'Daddy, is the Labour man the best one?' Sheila broke into the conversation again.

'Well I think so – of all the ones,' he answered.

'Then I'll pick the Labour man too,' she announced.

'You can't vote, stupid,' Sammy said, which caused a dismayed protest from his sister. 'Sure neither can I,' he went on. 'You have to be twenty-one.'

'I told you elections were for big people,' chipped in Mrs Dougan.

'Well, if Sheila and me are for the Labour man, that's not so bad. Sure there aren't many around here who are. I'll do the voting for both of us.' Sheila was delighted with this solution from her father. Her mother was scandalized yet again at her daughter's too early introduction to politics.

After tea, Sheila went to find her friends. There was too much expectancy among them to allow for play. The pending visit of the Unionist man was uppermost in their minds.

'D'ye think he'll be here soon?' asked Margaret.

'The car said seven o'clock. Sure it's nearly that now,' said Emily.

They were sitting on the kerbstone on the side of the road. Sheila picked up an old lollipop stick and began to dig in the cracks on the pavement. She had a burning question in her mind. Finally she asked it.

'What's your Daddy voting for?'

'Unionist,' replied Margaret. 'What's yours?'

'Labour.'

Margaret hooted in derision. 'You can't vote Labour. Nobody votes for Labour. They're no good.'

'Yes they are. My Daddy says they are. And you can so vote for Labour!' Sheila grew quite heated in her exchange of views with Margaret.

'Everybody votes for the Unionist man, don't they Emily?' Margaret turned to the other little girl for support. She conceded that nearly everybody did, and revealed her own parents' support to be for the same party.

'Hey – if your Daddy's Labour, that means you are too.' Margaret began to dance up and down, chanting, 'Sheila's a silly Labour,' over and over again until Emily suddenly announced that she could hear a band, which meant that the Unionist man must be coming. She and Margaret ran to tell their parents.

Sheila went towards her house too, but slowly, and deep in thought. She was considering her position as sole Labour supporter among her friends. She began to wish she had kept her mouth shut. Sheila was very puzzled by the whole thing. If it was true that everybody, or even nearly everybody, was picking the Unionist man, then maybe *he* was the best one, and not the Labour one. Even her Daddy had said not many people picked the Labour man. But her Daddy knew a lot of things and she felt he just couldn't be wrong. Everybody else must be wrong. There and then she made a momentous decision. When the Unionist man came and everybody was cheering him, as she was sure they would, she would boo very loudly. Just so that he would know that not everybody was for him. There was still the thorny problem of being the odd one out, but she pushed that to the back of her mind, as the band was very close now.

She ran into the house and asked her father if he was coming out to see everything. His reply that he wouldn't bother, he had heard it all before, puzzled her, but there was no time to ask him what he meant.

People were streaming from their houses as Sheila ran outside. They nodded greetings at each other, and little groups formed as the band marched towards them.

Behind the band was a big truck draped all over, it seemed, with swathes of red, white and blue material. The front was festooned with Union Jacks. Someone in the band blew a whistle. They stopped marching and playing, and the truck came to a halt behind them. Sheila and her friends made their way to the edge of the pavement, right in front of the crowd, beside the truck.

There were about a dozen people sitting in the back of the truck. The women all wore big hats with funny brims. The men were all in dark suits.

One man stood up to introduce the Unionist candidate, who then got to his feet amid claps and cheers. 'Now,' said a wee voice inside Sheila. But her nerve failed her. Margaret and Emily were jumping up and down beside her cheering their heads off. Perhaps I should be cheering too, Sheila was thinking. Everybody else is. But she just stood there quietly.

The Unionist man talked into the microphone. Every now and then he would say something which set everyone cheering and clapping again. He looked very pleased with himself, especially when he raised a cheer. Each time he did, though, Sheila faced her dilemma, and each time, she did nothing.

He finished his speech by picking up a small Union Jack. 'Remember,' he cried. 'This we will maintain.' He boomed out the slogan from the posters and the cheers crescendoed. All of a sudden, as if sparked by the only recognizable words she had heard, Sheila went into action. She began booing as loudly as her young lungs would allow.

'What're you doing?' yelled Margaret. She couldn't believe her eyes and ears.

'I'm booing,' said Sheila, quite unnecessarily, and carried on.

'Why?'

'Because!' The ultimate answer.

The Unionist man was beaming around him. He was waving at everyone. Margaret and Emily cheered all the louder. Sheila booed even harder. The Unionist man smiled down benignly on the three little girls. Sheila was engaged in taking a deep breath, and, unaware that the attention of the candidate had come to rest on them, let go the biggest boo she had managed so far. At one and the same moment, she noticed the Unionist man gazing down at her and her friends. She also noticed the smile freeze on his face as he realized that she was not cheering like the other two. It was only a fleeting reaction, but Sheila felt an overwhelming sense of victory and achievement.

He knows now, she thought gleefully to herself. He knows not *everybody* wants to pick him.

'He *saw* you!' gasped Margaret, aghast at the thought.

'I know, and sucks to him,' replied Sheila, and skipped back home to tell her Daddy all about it.

The Trout

SEAN O'FAOLAIN

One of the first places Julia always ran to when they arrived
in G— was The Dark Walk. It is a laurel walk, very old;
almost gone wild; a lofty midnight tunnel of smooth, sinewy
branches. Underfoot the tough brown leaves are never dry
enough to crackle: there is always a suggestion of damp and
cool trickle.

She raced right into it. For the first few yards she always had
the memory of the sun behind her, then she felt the dusk closing
swiftly down on her so that she screamed with pleasure and raced
on to reach the light at the far end; and it was always just a little
too long in coming so that she emerged gasping, clasping her
hands, laughing, drinking in the sun. When she was filled with
the heat and glare she would turn and consider the ordeal
again.

This year she had the extra joy of showing it to her small brother, and of terrifying him as well as herself. And for him the fear lasted longer because his legs were so short and she had gone out at the far end while he was still screaming and racing.

When they had done this many times they came back to the house to tell everybody that they had done it. He boasted. She mocked. They squabbled.

'Cry babby!'

'You were afraid yourself, so there!'

'I won't take you any more.'

'You're a big pig.'

'I hate you.'

Tears were threatening, so somebody said, 'Did you see the well?' She opened her eyes at that and held up her long lovely neck suspiciously and decided to be incredulous. She was twelve and at that age little girls are beginning to suspect most stories: they have already found out too many, from Santa Claus to the stork. How could there be a well! In The Dark Walk? That she had visited year after year? Haughtily she said, 'Nonsense.'

But she went back, pretending to be going somewhere else, and she found a hole scooped in the rock at the side of the walk, choked with damp leaves, so shrouded by ferns that she uncovered it only after much searching. At the back of this little cavern there was about a quart of water. In the water she suddenly perceived a panting trout. She rushed for Stephen and dragged him to see, and they were both so excited that they were no longer afraid of the darkness as they hunched down and peered in at the fish panting in his tiny prison, his silver stomach going up and down like an engine.

Nobody knew how the trout got there. Even old Martin in the kitchen garden laughed and refused to believe that it was there, or pretended not to believe, until she forced him to come down and see. Kneeling and pushing back his tattered old cap he peered in.

'Be cripes, you're right. How the divil in hell did that fella get there?'

She stared at him suspiciously.

'You knew?' she accused; but he said, 'The divil a' know,' and reached down to lift it out. Convinced, she hauled him back. If she had found it, then it was her trout.

Her mother suggested that a bird had carried the spawn. Her father thought that in the winter a small streamlet might have carried it down there as a baby, and it had been safe until the summer came and the water began to dry up. She said, 'I see,' and went back to look again and consider the matter in private. Her brother remained behind, wanting to hear the whole story of the trout, not really interested in the actual trout but much interested in the story which his mummy began to make up for him on the lines of, 'So one day Daddy Trout and Mammy Trout . . .' When he related it to her she said, 'Pooh.'

It troubled her that the trout was always in the same position; he had no room to turn; all the time the silver belly went up and down; otherwise he was motionless. She wondered what he ate, and in between visits to Joey Pony and the boat, and a bathe to get cool, she thought of his hunger. She brought him down bits of dough; once she brought him a worm. He ignored the food. He just went on panting. Hunched over him she thought how all the winter, while she was at school, he had been in there. All the winter, in The Dark Walk, all day, all night, floating around alone. She drew the leaf of her hat down around her ears and chin and stared. She was still thinking of it as she lay in bed.

It was late June, the longest days of the year. The sun had sat still for a week, burning up the world. Although it was after ten o'clock it was still bright and still hot. She lay on her back under a single sheet, with her long legs spread, trying to keep cool. She could see the D of the moon through the fir tree – they slept on the ground floor. Before they went to bed her mummy had told Stephen the story of the trout again, and she, in her bed, had resolutely presented her back to them and read her book. But she had kept one ear cocked.

'And so, in the end, this naughty fish who would not stay at home got bigger and bigger and bigger, and the water got smaller and smaller . . .'

Passionately she had whirled and cried, 'Mummy, don't make it a horrible old moral story!' Her mummy had brought in a fairy godmother then, who sent lots of rain, and filled the well, and a stream poured out and the trout floated away down to the river below. Staring at the moon she knew that there are no such things as fairy godmothers and that the trout, down in The Dark Walk, was panting like an engine. She heard somebody unwind a fishing reel. Would the *beasts* fish him out!

She sat up. Stephen was a hot lump of sleep, lazy thing. The Dark Walk would be full of little scraps of moon. She leaped up and looked out the window, and somehow it was not so lightsome now that she saw the dim mountains far away and the black firs against the breathing land and heard a dog say *bark-bark*. Quietly she lifted the ewer of water and climbed out the window and scuttled along the cool but cruel gravel down to the maw of the tunnel. Her pyjamas were very short so that when she splashed water it wet her ankles. She peered into the tunnel. Something alive rustled inside there. She raced in, and up and down she raced, and flurried, and cried aloud, 'Oh, gosh, I can't find it,' and then at last she did. Kneeling down in the damp she put her hand into the slimy hole. When the body lashed they were both mad with fright. But she gripped him and shoved him into the ewer and raced, with her teeth ground, out to the other end of the tunnel and down the steep paths to the river's edge.

All the time she could feel him lashing his tail against the side of the ewer. She was afraid he would jump right out. The gravel cut into her soles until she came to the cool ooze of the river's bank where the moon mice on the water crept into her feet. She poured out, watching until he plopped. For a second he was visible in the water. She hoped he was not dizzy. Then all she saw was the glimmer of the moon in the silent-flowing river, the dark firs, the dim mountains, and the radiant pointed face laughing down at her out of the empty sky.

She scuttled up the hill, in the window, plonked down the ewer, and flew through the air like a bird into bed. The dog said *bark-bark*. She heard the fishing reel whirring. She hugged herself and giggled. Like a river of joy her holiday spread before her.

In the morning Stephen rushed to her, shouting that 'he' was gone, and asking 'where' and 'how'. Lifting her nose in the air she said superciliously, 'Fairy godmother, I suppose?' and strolled away patting the palms of her hands.

Three Lambs

LIAM O'FLAHERTY

Little Michael rose before dawn. He tried to make as little
noise as possible. He ate two slices of bread and butter and
drank a cup of milk, although he hated cold milk with bread
and butter in the morning. But on an occasion like this, what
did it matter what a boy ate? He was going out to watch the
black sheep having a lamb. His father had mentioned the night
before that the black sheep was sure to lamb that morning,
and of course there was a prize, three pancakes, for the first
one who saw the lamb.

He lifted the latch gently and stole out. It was best not to let his brother John know he was going. He would be sure to want to come too. As he ran down the lane, his sleeves, brushing against the evergreen bushes, were wetted by the dew, and the tip of his cap was just visible above the hedge, bobbing up and down as he ran. He was in too great a hurry to open the gate and tore a little hole in the breast of his blue jersey climbing over it. But he didn't mind that. He would get another one on his thirteenth birthday.

He turned to the left from the main road, up a lane that led to the field where his father, the magistrate, kept his prize sheep. It was only a quarter of a mile, that lane, but he thought that it would never end and he kept tripping among the stones that strewed the road. It was so awkward to run on the stones wearing shoes, and it was too early in the year yet to be allowed to go barefooted. He envied Little Jimmy, the son of the farm labourer, who was allowed to go barefooted all the year round, even in the depths of winter, and who always had such wonderful cuts on his big toes, the envy of all the little boys in the village school.

He climbed over the fence leading into the fields and, clapping his hands together, said, 'Oh, you devil,' a swear word he had learned from Little Jimmy and of which he was very proud. He took off his shoes and stockings and hid them in a hole in the fence. Then he ran jumping, his bare heels looking like round brown spots as he tossed them up behind him. The grass was wet and the ground was hard, but he persuaded himself that it was great fun.

Going through a gap into the next field, he saw a rabbit nibbling grass. He halted suddenly, his heart beating loudly. Pity he hadn't a dog. The rabbit stopped eating. He cocked up his ears. He stood on his tail, with his neck craned up and his fore feet hanging limp. Then he came down again. He thrust his ears forward. Then he lay flat with his ears buried in his back and lay still. With a great yell Little Michael darted forward imitating a dog barking and the rabbit scurried away in short sharp leaps. Only his white tail was visible in the grey light.

Little Michael went into the next field, but the sheep were nowhere to be seen. He stood on a hillock and called out 'Chowin, chowin,' three times. Then he heard 'Mah-m-m-m' in the next field and ran on. The sheep were in the last two fields, two oblong little fields, running in a hollow between two crags, surrounded by high thick fences, the walls of an old fort. In the nearest of the two fields he found ten of the sheep, standing side by side, looking at him, with their fifteen lambs in front of them also looking at him curiously. He counted them out loud and then he saw that the black sheep was not there. He panted with excitement. Perhaps she already had a lamb in the next field. He hurried to the gap leading into the next field, walking stealthily, avoiding the spots where the grass was high, so as to make less noise. It was bad to disturb a sheep that was lambing. He peered through a hole in the fence and could see nothing. Then he crawled to the gap and peered around the corner. The black sheep was just inside standing with her fore feet on a little mound.

Her belly was swollen out until it ended on each side in a sharp point and her legs appeared to be incapable of supporting her body. She turned her head sharply and listened. Little Michael held his breath, afraid to make a noise. It was of vital importance not to disturb the sheep. Straining back to lie down he burst a button on his trousers and he knew his braces were undone. He said, 'Oh, you devil,' again and decided to ask his mother to let him wear a belt instead of braces, same as Little Jimmy wore. Then he crawled farther back from the gap and taking off his braces altogether made it into a belt. It hurt his hips, but he felt far better and manly.

Then he came back again to the gap and looked. The black sheep was still in the same place. She was scratching the earth with her fore feet and going around in a circle, as if she wanted to lie down but was afraid to lie down. Sometimes she ground her teeth and made an awful noise, baring her jaws and turning her head around sideways. Little Michael felt a pain in his heart in pity for her, and he wondered why the other sheep didn't come to keep her company. Then he wondered whether his mother had felt the same pain when she had Ethna the autumn before. She must have, because the doctor was there.

Suddenly the black sheep went on her knees. She stayed a few seconds on her knees and then she moaned and sank to the ground and stretched herself out with her neck on the little hillock and her hind quarters falling down the little slope. Little Michael forgot about the pain now. His heart thumped with excitement. He forgot to breathe, looking intently. 'Ah,' he said. The sheep stretched again and struggled to her feet and circled around once stamping and grinding her teeth. Little Michael moved up to her slowly. She looked at him anxiously, but she was too sick to move away. He broke the bladder and he saw two little feet sticking out. He seized them carefully and pulled. The sheep moaned again and pressed with all her might. The lamb dropped on the grass.

Little Michael sighed with delight and began to rub its body with his finger nails furiously. The sheep turned around and smelt it, making a funny happy noise in its throat. The lamb, its white body covered with yellow slime, began to move, and presently it tried to stand up, but it fell again and Little Michael kept rubbing it, sticking his fingers into its ears and nostrils to clear them. He was so intent on this work that he did not notice the sheep had moved away again, and it was only when the lamb was able to stand up and he wanted to give it suck, that he noticed the sheep was lying again giving birth to another lamb. 'Oh, you devil,' gasped Little Michael, 'six pancakes.'

The second lamb was white like the first but with a black spot on its right ear. Little Michael rubbed it vigorously, pausing now and again to help the first lamb to its feet as it tried to stagger about. The sheep circled around making low noises in her throat, putting her nostrils to each lamb in turn, stopping nowhere, as giddy as a young school girl, while the hard pellets of earth that stuck to her belly jingled like beads when she moved. Little Michael then took the first lamb and tried to put it to suck, but it refused to take the teat, stupidly sticking its mouth into the wool. Then he put his finger in its mouth and gradually got the teat in with his other hand. Then he pressed the teat and the hot milk squirted into the lamb's mouth. The lamb shook its tail, shrugged its body, made a little drive with its head and began to suck.

Little Michael was just going to give the second lamb suck, when the sheep moaned and moved away again. He said 'chowin, chowin, poor chowin,' and put the lamb to her head, but she turned away moaning and grinding her teeth and stamping. 'Oh, you devil,' said Little Michael, 'she is going to have another lamb.'

The sheep lay down again, with her fore leg stretched out in front of her and, straining her neck backwards, gave birth to a third lamb, a black lamb.

Then she rose smartly to her feet, her two sides hollow now. She shrugged herself violently and, without noticing the lambs, started to eat grass fiercely, just pausing now and again to say 'mah-m-m-m.'

Little Michael, in an ecstasy of delight, rubbed the black lamb until it was able to stand. Then he put all the lambs to suck, the sheep eating around her in a circle, without changing her feet, smelling a lamb now and again. 'Oh, you devil,' Little Michael kept saying, thinking he would be quite famous now, and talked about for a whole week. It was not every day that a sheep had three lambs.

He brought them to a sheltered spot under the fence. He wiped the birth slime from his hands with some grass. He opened his penknife and cut the dirty wool from the sheep's udder, lest the lambs might swallow some and die. Then he gave a final look at them, said, 'Chowin, Chowin,' tenderly and turned to go.

He was already at the gap when he stopped with a start.

He raced back to the lambs and examined each of them. 'Three she lambs,' he gasped. 'Oh, you devil, that never happened before. Maybe father will give me half a crown.'

And as he raced homeward, he barked like a dog in his delight.

My Vocation

MARY LAVIN

I'm not married yet, but I'm still in hopes. One thing is certain though: I was never cut out to be a nun in the first place. Anyway, I was only thirteen when I got the Call, and I think if we were living out here in Crumlin at the time, in the new houses that the Government gave us, I'd never have got it at all, because we hardly ever see nuns out here, somehow, and a person wouldn't take so much notice of them out here anyway. It's so airy you know, and they blow along in their big white bonnets and a person wouldn't take any more notice of them than the seagulls that blow in from the sea. And then, too, you'd never get near enough to them out here to get the smell of them.

It was the smell of them I used to love in the Dorset Street days, when they'd stop us in the street to talk to us, when we'd be playing hopscotch on the path. I used to push up as close to them as possible and take big sniffs of them. But that was nothing to when they came up to the room to see Mother. You'd get it terribly strong then.

'What smell are you talking about?' said my father one day when I was going on about them after they went. 'That's no way to talk about people in Religious Orders,' he said. 'There's no smell at all off the like of them.'

That was right, of course, and I saw where I was wrong. It was the no-smell that I used to get, but there were so many smells fighting for place in Dorset Street, fried onions, and garbage, and the smell of old rags, that a person with no smell at all stood out a mile from everybody else. Anyone with an eye in their head could see that I didn't mean any disrespect. It vexed me shockingly to have my father think such a thing. I told him so, too, straight out.

'And if you want to know,' I finished up, 'I'm going to be a nun myself when I get big.'

But my father only roared laughing.

'Do you hear that?' he said, turning to Mother. 'Isn't that a good one? She'll be joining the same order as you, I'm thinking.' And he roared out laughing again: a very common laugh I thought, even though he was my father.

And he was nothing to my brother Paudeen.

'We'll be all right if it isn't the Order of Mary Magdalen that one joins,' he said.

What do you make of that for commonness? Is it any wonder I wanted to get away from the lot of them?

He was always at me, that fellow, saying I was cheapening myself, and telling Ma on me if he saw me as much as lift my eye to a fellow passing me in the street.

'She's mad for boys, that one,' he used to say. And it wasn't true at all. It wasn't my fault if the boys were always after me, was it? And even if I felt a bit sparky now and then, wasn't

89

that the kind that always became nuns? I never saw a plain-looking one, did you? I never did. Not in those days, I mean. The ones that used to come visiting us in Dorset Street were all gorgeous-looking, with pale faces and not a rotten tooth in their heads. They were twice as good-looking as the Tiller Girls in the Gaiety. And on Holy Thursday, when we were doing the Seven Churches, and we used to cross over the Liffey to the south side to make up the number, I used to go into the Convent of the Reparation just to look at the nuns. You see them inside in a kind of little golden cage, back of the altar in their white habits with blue sashes and their big silver beads dangling down by their side. They were like angels: honest to God. You'd be sure of it if you didn't happen to hear them give an odd cough now and again, or a sneeze.

It was in there with them I'd like to be, but Sis – she's my girl friend – she told me they were all ladies, titled ladies too, some of them, and I'd have to be a lay sister. I wasn't having any of that, thank you. I could have gone away to domestic service any day if that was only all the ambition I had. It would have broken my mother's heart to see me scrubbing floors and the like. She never sank that low, although there were fourteen of them in the family, and only eleven of us. She was never anything less than a wards' maid in the Mater Hospital, and they're sort of nurses, if you like, and when she met my father she was after getting an offer of a great job as a barmaid in Geary's of Parnell Street. She'd never have held with me being a lay sister.

'I don't hold with there being any such things as lay sisters at all,' she said. 'They're not allowed a hot jar in their beds, I believe, and they have to sit at the back of the chapel with no red plush on their kneeler. If you ask me, it's a queer thing to see the Church making distinctions.'

She had a great regard for the Orders that had no lay sisters at all, like the Little Sisters of the Poor, and the Visiting Sisters.

'Oh, they're the grand women!' she said.

You'd think then, wouldn't you, that she'd be glad when I decided to join them. But she was as much against me as any of them.

'Is it you?' she cried. 'You'd want to get the impudent look taken off your face if that's the case!' she said, tightly.

I suppose it was the opposition that nearly drove me mad. It made me dead set on going ahead with the thing.

You see, they never went against me in any of the things I was going to be before that. The time I said I was going to be a Tiller Girl in the Gaiety, you should have seen the way they went on: all of them. They were dead keen on the idea.

'Are you tall enough though – that's the thing?' said Paudeen.

And the tears came into my mother's eyes.

'That's what I always wanted to be when I was a girl,' she said, and she dried her eyes and turned to my father. 'Do you think there is anyone you could ask to use his influence?' she said. Because she was always sure and certain that influence was the only thing that would get you any job.

But it wasn't influence in the Tiller Girls: it was legs. And I knew that, and my legs were never my strong point, so I gave up that idea.

Then there was the time I thought I'd like to be a waitress, even though I wasn't a blonde, said Paudeen morosely.

But you should see the way they went on then too.

'A packet of henna would soon settle the hair question,' said my mother.

'Although I'm sure some waitresses are good girls,' she said. 'It all depends on a girl herself, and the kind of a home she comes from.'

They were doubtful if I'd get any of these jobs, but they didn't raise any obstacles, and they didn't laugh at me like they did in this case.

'And what will I do for money,' said my father, 'when they come looking for your dowry? If you haven't an education you have to have money, going into those convents.'

But I turned a deaf ear to him.

'The Lord will provide,' I said. 'If it's His will for me to be a nun He'll find a way out of all difficulties,' I said grandly, and in a voice I imagined to be as near as I could make it to the ladylike voices of the Visiting Sisters.

But I hadn't much hope of getting into the Visiting Sisters. To begin with, they always seemed to take it for granted I'd get married.

'I hope you're a good girl,' they used to say to me, and you'd know by the way they said it what they meant. 'Boys may like a fast girl when it comes to having a good time, but it's the modest girl they pick when it comes to choosing a wife,' they said. And such-like things. They were always harping on the one string. Sure they'd never get over it if I told them what I had in mind. I'd never have the face to tell them!

And then one day what did I see but an advertisement in the paper.

'Wanted, Postulants,' it said, in big letters, and then underneath in small letters, there was the address of the Reverend Mother you were to apply to, and in smaller letters still, at the very bottom, were the words that made me sit up and take notice: 'No Dowry,' they said.

'That's me,' said I, and there and then I up and wrote off to them, without as much as saying a word to anyone only Sis.

Poor Sis: you should have seen how bad she took it.

'I can't believe it,' she said over and over again, and she threw her arms around me and burst out crying. She was always a good sort, Sis.

Every time she looked at me she burst out crying. And I must say that was more like the way I expected people to take me. But as a matter of fact Sis started the ball rolling, and it wasn't long after that everyone began to feel bad, because you see, the next thing that happened was a telegram arrived from the Reverend Mother in answer to my letter.

'It can't be for you,' said my mother, as she ripped it open. 'Who'd be sending you a telegram?'

And I didn't know who could have sent it either until I read the signature. It was Sister Mary Alacoque.

That was the name of the nun in the paper.

'It's for me all right,' I said then. 'I wrote to her,' I said and I felt a bit awkward.

My mother grabbed back the telegram.

'Glory be to God!' she said, but I don't think she meant it as a prayer. 'Do you see what it says? "Calling to see you this afternoon. *Deo Gratias*." What on earth is the meaning of all this?'

'Well,' I said defiantly, 'when I told you I was going to be a nun you wouldn't believe me. Maybe you'll believe it when I'm out among the savages!' I added. Because it was a missionary order: that's why they didn't care about the dowry. People are always leaving money in their wills to the Foreign Missions, and you don't need to be too highly educated to teach savages, I suppose.

'Glory be to God!' said my mother again. And then she turned on me. 'Get up out of that and we'll try and put some sort of front on things before they get here: there'll be two of them, I'll swear. Nuns never go out alone. Hurry up, will you?'

Never in your life did you see anyone carry on like my mother did that day. For the few hours that remained of the morning she must have worked like a lunatic, running mad around the room, shoving things under the bed, and ramming home the drawers of the chest, and sweeping things off the seats of the chairs.

'They'll want to see a chair they can sit on, anyway,' she said. 'And I suppose we'll have to offer them a bite to eat.'

'Oh, a cup of tea,' said my father.

But my mother had very grand ideas at times.

'Oh, I always heard you should give monks or nuns a good meal,' she said. 'They can eat things out in the world that they can't eat in the convent. As long as you don't ask them. Don't say will you or won't you! Just set it in front of them – that's what I always heard.'

I will say this for my mother, she has a sense of occasion, because we never heard any of this lore when the Visiting Sisters called, or even the Begging Sisters, although you'd think they could do with a square meal by the look of them sometimes.

But no: there was never before seen such a fuss as she made on this occasion.

'Run out to Mrs Mullins in the front room and ask her for the lend of her brass fender,' she cried, giving me a push out of the door. 'And see if poor Mr Duffy is home from work – he'll be good enough to let us have a chair, I'm sure, the poor soul, the one with the plush seat,' she cried, coming out to the landing after me, and calling across the well of the stairs.

As I disappeared into Mrs Mullins' I could see her standing in the doorway as if she was trying to make up her mind about something. And sure enough, when I came out lugging the fender with me, she ran across and took it from me.

'Run down to the return room, like a good child,' she said, 'and ask old Mrs Dooley for her tablecloth – the one with the lace edging she got from America.' And as I showed some reluctance, she caught my arm. 'You might give her a wee hint of what's going on. Won't everyone know it as soon as the nuns arrive, and it'll give her the satisfaction of having the news ahead of everyone else.'

But it would be hard to say who had the news first because I was only at the foot of the steps leading to the return room when I could hear doors opening in every direction on our own landing, and the next minute you'd swear they were playing a new kind of postman's knock, in which each one carried a piece of furniture round with him, by the way our friends and neighbours were rushing back and forth across the landing; old Ma Dunne with her cuckoo clock, and young Mrs McBride, that shouldn't be carrying heavy things at all, with our old wicker chair that she was going to exchange for the time with a new one of her own. And I believe she wanted to get her piano rolled in to us too, only there wasn't time!

That was the great thing about Dorset Street: you could meet any and all occasions, you had so many friends at your back. And you could get anything you wanted, all in a few minutes, without anyone outside the landing being any the wiser.

My mother often said it was like one big happy family, that landing – including the return room, of course.

The only thing was everyone wanted to have a look at the room.

We'll never get shut of them before the nuns arrive, I thought.

'Isn't this the great news entirely,' said old Mrs Dooley, making her way up the stairs as soon as I told her. And she rushed up to my mother and kissed her. 'Not but that you deserve it,' she said. 'I never knew a priest or a nun yet that hadn't a good mother behind them!' And then Mrs McBride coming out, she drew her into it. 'Isn't that so, Mrs McBride?' she cried. 'I suppose you heard the news?'

'I did indeed,' said Mrs McBride. 'Not that I was surprised,' she said, but I think she only wanted to let on she was greater with us than she was, because as Sis could tell you, there was nothing of the Holy Molly about me – far from it.

What old Mr Duffy said was more like what you'd expect.

'Well, doesn't that beat all!' he cried, hearing the news as he came up the last step of the stairs. 'Ah, well, I always heard it's the biggest divils that make the best saints, and now I can believe it!'

He was a terribly nice old man.

'And is it the Foreign Missions?' he asked, calling me to one side, 'because if that's the case I want you to know you can send me raffle tickets for every draw you hold, and I'll sell the lot for you and get the stubs back in good time, with the money along with it in postal orders. And what's more –' he was going on, when Mrs Mullins let out a scream:

'You didn't tell me it was the Missions,' she cried. 'Oh, God help you, you poor child!' And she threw up her hands. 'How will any of us be saved at all at all with the like of you going to the ends of the earth where you'll never see a living soul only blacks till the day you die! Oh, glory be to God. And to think we never knew who we had in our midst!'

In some ways it was what I expected, but in another way I'd have liked if they didn't all look at me in such a pitying way.

And old Mrs Dooley put the lid on it.

'A saint – that's what you are, child,' she cried, and she caught my hand and pulled me down close to her – she was a low butt of a little woman. 'They tell me it's out to the poor lepers you're going?'

That was the first I heard about lepers, I can tell you. And I partly guessed the poor old thing had picked it up wrong, but all the same I put a knot in my handkerchief to remind me to ask where I was going.

And I may as well admit straight out, that I wasn't having anything to do with any lepers. I hadn't thought of backing out of the thing entirely at that time, but I was backing out of it if it was to be lepers!

The thought of the lepers gave me the creeps, I suppose. Did you ever get the feeling when a thing was mentioned that you *had* it? Well, that was the way I felt. I kept going over to the basin behind the screen (Mrs McBride's) and washing my hands every minute, and as for spitting out, my throat was raw by the time I heard the cab at the door.

'Here they come,' cried my father, raising his hand like the starter at the dog track.

'Out of this, all of you,' cried Mrs Mullins, rushing out and giving an example to everyone.

'Holy God!' said my mother, but I don't think that was meant to be a prayer either.

But she had nothing to be uneasy about: the room was gorgeous.

That was another thing: I thought they'd be delighted with the room. We never did it up any way special for the Visiting Sisters, but they were always saying how nice we kept it: maybe that was only to encourage my mother, but all the same it was very nice of them. But when the two Recruiting Officers arrived (it was my father called them that after they went), they didn't seem to notice the room at all in spite of what we'd done to it.

And do you know what I heard one of them say to the other?

'It seems clean, anyway,' she said.

Now I didn't like that 'seems'. And what did she mean by the 'anyway' I'd like to know?

It sort of put me off from the start – would you believe that? That, and the look of them. They weren't a bit like the Visiting Sisters – or even the Begging Sisters; who all had lovely figures – like statues. One of them was thin all right, but I didn't like the look of her all the same. She didn't look thin in an ordinary way; she looked worn away, if you know what I mean? And the other one was fat. She was so fat I was afraid if she fell on the stairs she'd start to roll like a ball.

She was the boss: the fat one.

And do you know one of the first things she asked me? You'd never guess. I don't even like to mention it. She caught a hold of my hair.

'I hope you keep it nice and clean,' she said.

What do you think of that? I was glad my mother didn't hear her. My mother forgets herself entirely if she's mad about anything. She didn't hear it, though. But I began to think to myself that they must have met some very low-class girls if they had to ask *that* question. And wasn't that what you'd think?

Then the worn-looking one said a queer thing, not to me, but to the other nun.

'She seems strong, anyway,' she said. And there again I don't think she meant my health. I couldn't help putting her remark alongside the way she was so worn-looking; and I began to think I'd got myself into a nice pickle.

But I was prepared to go through with it all the same. That's me: I have great determination although you mightn't believe it. Sis often says I'd have been well able for the savages if I'd gone on with the thing.

But I didn't.

I missed it by a hair's breadth, though. I won't tell you all the interview, but at the end of it anyway they gave me the name of the Convent where I was to go for Probation, and they told me the day to go, and they gave me a list of clothes I was to get.

'Will you be able to pay for them?' they said, turning to my father. They hadn't taken much notice of him up to that.

I couldn't help admiring the way he answered.

'Well, I managed to pay for plenty of style for her up to now,' he said, 'and seeing that this mourning outfit is to be the last I'll be asked to pay for, I think I'll manage it all right. Why?'

I admired the 'why?'

'Oh, we have to be ready for all eventualities,' said the fat one.

Sis and I nearly died laughing afterwards thinking of those words. But I hardly noticed them at the time, because I was on my way out the door to order a cab. They had asked me to get one and they had given me so many instructions that I was nearly daft.

They didn't want a flighty horse, and they didn't want a cab that was too high up off the ground, and I was to pick a cabby that looked respectable.

Now at this time, although there were still cabs to be hired, you didn't have an almighty great choice, and I knew I had my work cut out for me to meet all their requirements.

But I seemed to be dead in luck in more ways than one, because when I went to the cab stand there, among the shiny black cabs, with big black horses that rolled their eyes at me, there was one old cab and it was all battered and green-mouldy. The cabby too looked about as mouldy as the cab. And as for the horse – well, wouldn't anyone think that he'd be mouldy too. But as a matter of fact the horse wasn't mouldy in any way. Indeed, it was due to the way he bucketed it about that the old cab was so racked-looking: it was newer than the others I believe, and as for the cabby, I believe it was the horse had him so bad-looking. That horse had the heart scalded in him.

But it was only afterwards I heard all this. I thought I'd done great work, and I went up and got the nuns, and put them into it and off they went, with the thin one waving to me.

It was while I was still waving that I saw the horse starting his capers.

My first thought was to run, but I thought I'd have to face them again, so I didn't do that. Instead, I ran after the cab and shouted to the driver to stop.

Perhaps that was what did the damage. Maybe I drove the horse clean mad altogether, because the next thing he reared up and let his hind legs fly. There was a dreadful crash and a sound of splintering, and the next thing I knew the bottom of the cab came down on the road with a clatter. I suppose it had got such abuse from that animal from time to time it was on the point of giving way all the time.

It was a miracle for them they weren't let down on the road – the two nuns. It was a miracle for me too in another way because if they did I'd have to go and pick them up and I'd surely be drawn deeper into the whole thing.

But that wasn't what happened. Off went the horse, as mad as ever down the street, rearing and leaping, but the nuns must have got a bit of a warning and held on to the sides, because the next thing I saw, along with the set of four feet under the horse, was four more feet showing out under the body of the cab, and running for dear life.

Honest to God, I started to laugh. Wasn't that awful? They

could have been killed, and I knew it, although as a matter of fact someone caught hold of the cab before it got to Parnell Street and they were taken out of it and put into another cab. But once I started to laugh I couldn't stop, and in a way – if you can understand such a thing – I laughed away my vocation. Wasn't that awful?

Not but that I have a great regard for nuns even to this day, although mind you, I sometimes think the nuns that are going nowadays are not the same as the nuns that were going in our Dorset Street days. I saw a terribly plain-looking one the other day in Cabra Avenue. But all the same, they're grand women! I'm going to make a point of sending all my kids to school with the nuns anyway, when I have them. But of course it takes a fellow with a bit of money to educate his kids nowadays. A girl has to have an eye to the future, as I always tell Sis – she's my girl friend, you remember.

Well, we're going out to Dollymount this afternoon, Sis and me, and you'd never know who we'd pick up. So long for the present!

The Genius

FRANK O'CONNOR

Some kids are cissies by nature but I was a cissy by conviction. Mother had told me about geniuses; I wanted to be one, and I could see for myself that fighting, as well as being sinful, was dangerous. The kids round the Barrack where I lived were always fighting. Mother said they were savages, that I needed proper friends, and that once I was old enough to go to school I would meet them.

My way, when someone wanted to fight and I could not get away, was to climb on the nearest wall and argue like hell in a shrill voice about Our Blessed Lord and good manners. This was a way of attracting attention, and it usually worked because the enemy, having stared incredulously at me for several minutes, wondering if he would have time to hammer my head on the pavement before someone came out to him, yelled something like 'blooming cissy' and went away in disgust. I didn't like being called a cissy but I preferred it to fighting. I felt very like one of those poor mongrels who slunk through our neighbourhood and took to their heels when anyone came near them, and I always tried to make friends with them.

I toyed with games, and enjoyed kicking a ball gently before me along the pavement till I discovered that any boy who joined me grew violent and started to shoulder me out of the way. I preferred little girls because they didn't fight so much, but otherwise I found them insipid and lacking in any solid basis of information. The only women I cared for were grown-ups, and my most intimate friend was an old washerwoman called Miss Cooney who had been in the lunatic asylum and was very religious. It was she who had told me all about dogs. She would run a mile after anyone she saw hurting an animal, and even went to the police about them, but the police knew she was mad and paid no attention.

She was a sad-looking woman with grey hair, high cheek-bones and toothless gums. While she ironed, I would sit for hours in the hot, steaming, damp kitchen, turning over the pages of her religious books. She was fond of me too, and told me she was sure I would be a priest. I agreed that I might be a bishop, but she didn't seem to think so highly of bishops. I told her there were so many other things I might be that I couldn't make up my mind, but she only smiled at this. Miss Cooney thought there was only one thing a genius could be and that was a priest.

On the whole I thought an explorer was what I would be. Our house was in a square between two roads, one terraced above the other, and I could leave home, follow the upper road for a mile past the Barrack, turn left on any of the in-tervening roads and lanes, and return almost without leaving the pavement. It was astonishing what valuable information you could pick up on a trip like that. When I came home I wrote down my adventures in a book called *The Voyages of Johnson Martin*, 'with many Maps and Illustrations, Irishtown University Press, 3s. 6d. nett'. I was also compiling *The Irishtown University Song Book for Use in Schools and Institutions by Johnson Martin*, which had the words and music of my favourite songs. I could not read music yet but I copied it from anything that came handy, preferring staff to solfa because it looked better on the page. But I still wasn't sure what I would be. All I knew was that I intended to be famous and have a statue put up to me near that of Father Matthew, in Patrick Street. Father Matthew was called the Apostle of Temperance, but I didn't think much of temperance. So far our town hadn't a proper genius and I intended to supply the deficiency.

But my work continued to bring home to me the great gaps in my knowledge. Mother understood my difficulty and worried herself endlessly finding answers to my questions, but neither she nor Miss Cooney had a great store of the sort of information I needed, and Father was more a hindrance than a help. He was talkative enough about subjects that interested himself but they did not greatly interest me. 'Ballybeg,' he would say brightly. 'Market town. Population 648. Nearest station, Rathkeale.' He was also forthcoming enough about other things, but later, Mother would take me aside and explain that he was only joking again. This made me mad, because I never knew when he was joking and when he wasn't.

I can see now, of course, that he didn't really like me. It was not the poor man's fault. He had never expected to be the father of a genius and it filled him with forebodings. He looked round him at all his contemporaries who had normal, bloodthirsty, illiterate children, and shuddered at the thought that I would never be good for anything but being a genius. To give him his due, it wasn't himself he worried about, but there had never been anything like it in the family before and he dreaded the shame of it. He would come in from the front door with his cap over his eyes and his hands in his trouser pockets and stare moodily at me while I sat at the kitchen table, surrounded by papers, producing fresh maps and illustrations for my book of voyages, or copying the music of 'The Minstrel Boy'.

'Why can't you go out and play with the Horgans?' he would ask wheedlingly, trying to make it sound attractive.

'I don't like the Horgans, Daddy,' I would reply politely.

'But what's wrong with them?' he would ask testily. 'They're fine manly young fellows.'

'They're always fighting, Daddy.'

'And what harm is fighting? Can't you fight them back?'

'I don't like fighting, Daddy, thank you,' I would say, still with perfect politeness.

'The dear knows, the child is right,' Mother would say, coming to my defence. 'I don't know what sort those children are.'

'Ah, you have him as bad as yourself,' Father would snort, and stalk to the front door again, to scald his heart with thoughts of the nice natural son he might have had if only he hadn't married the wrong woman. Granny had always said Mother was the wrong woman for him and now she was being proved right.

She was being proved so right that the poor man couldn't keep his eyes off me, waiting for the insanity to break out in me. One of the things he didn't like was my Opera House. The Opera House was a cardboard box I had mounted on two chairs in the dark hallway. It had a proscenium cut in it, and I had painted some back-drops of mountain and sea with wings that represented trees and rocks. The characters were pictures cut out, mounted and coloured, and moved on bits of stick. It was lit with candles, for which I had made coloured screens, greased so that they were transparent, and I made up operas from story-books and bits of songs. I was singing a passionate duet for two of the characters while twiddling the screens to produce the effect of moonlight when one of the screens caught fire and everything went up in a mass of flames. I screamed and Father came out to stamp out the blaze, and he cursed me till even Mother lost her temper with him and told him he was worse than six children, after which he wouldn't speak to her for a week.

Another time I was so impressed with a lame teacher I knew that I decided to have a lame leg myself, and there was hell in the home for days because Mother had no difficulty at all in seeing that my foot was already out of shape while Father only looked at it and sniffed contemptuously. I was furious with him, and Mother decided he wasn't much better than a monster. They quarrelled for days over that until it became quite an embarrassment to me because, though I was bored stiff with limping, I felt I should be letting her down by getting better. When I went down the Square, lurching from side to side, Father stood at the gate, looking after me with a malicious knowing smile, and when I had discarded my limp, the way he mocked Mother was positively disgusting.

2

As I say, they squabbled endlessly about what I should be told. Father was for telling me nothing.

'But, Mick,' Mother would say earnestly, 'the child must learn.'

'He'll learn soon enough when he goes to school,' he snarled. 'Why do you be always at him, putting ideas into his head? Isn't he bad enough? I'd sooner the boy would grow up a bit natural.'

But either Mother didn't like children to be natural or she thought I was natural enough, as I was. Women, of course, don't object to geniuses half as much as men do. I suppose they find them a relief.

Now one of the things I wanted badly to know was where babies came from, but this was something that no one seemed to be able to explain to me. When I asked Mother she got upset and talked about birds and flowers, and I decided that if she had ever known she must have forgotten it and was ashamed to say so. Miss Cooney only smiled wistfully when I asked her and said, 'You'll know all about that soon enough, child.'

'But, Miss Cooney,' I said with great dignity, 'I have to know now. It's for my work, you see.'

'Keep your innocence while you can, child,' she said in the same tone. 'Soon enough the world will rob you of it, and once 'tis gone 'tis gone for ever.'

But whatever the world wanted to rob me of, it was welcome to it from my point of view, if only I could get a few facts to work on. I appealed to Father and he told me that babies were dropped out of aeroplanes and if you caught one you could keep it. 'By parachute?' I asked, but he only looked pained and said, 'Oh, no, you don't want to begin by spoiling them.' Afterwards, Mother took me aside again and explained that he was only joking. I went quite dotty with rage and told her that one of these days he would go too far with his jokes.

All the same, it was a great worry to Mother. It wasn't every mother who had a genius for a son, and she dreaded that she might be wronging me. She suggested timidly to Father that he should tell me something about it and he danced with rage. I heard them because I was supposed to be playing with the Opera House upstairs at the time. He said she was going out of her mind, and that she was driving me out of my mind at the same time. She was very upset because she had considerable respect for his judgement.

At the same time when it was a matter of duty she could be very, very obstinate. It was a heavy responsibility, and she disliked it intensely – a deeply pious woman who never mentioned the subject at all to anybody if she could avoid it – but it had to be done. She took an awful long time over it – it was a summer day, and we were sitting on the bank of a stream in the Glen – but at last I managed to detach the fact that mummies had an engine in their tummies and daddies had a starting-handle that made it work, and once it started it went on until it made a baby. That certainly explained an awful lot of things I had not understood up to this – for instance, why fathers were necessary and why Mother had buffers on her chest while Father had none. It made her almost as interesting as a locomotive, and for days I went round deploring my own rotten luck that I wasn't a girl and couldn't have an engine and buffers of my own instead of a measly old starting-handle like Father.

Soon afterwards I went to school and disliked it intensely. I was too small to be moved up to the big boys and the other 'infants' were still at the stage of spelling 'cat' and 'dog'. I tried to tell the old teacher about my work, but she only smiled and said, 'Hush, Larry!' I hated being told to hush. Father was always saying it to me.

One day I was standing at the playground gate, feeling very lonely and dissatisfied, when a tall girl from the senior girls' school spoke to me. She was a girl with a plump, dark face and black pigtails.

'What's your name, little boy?' she asked.

I told her.

'Is this your first time at school?' she asked.

'Yes.'

'And do you like it?'

'No, I hate it,' I replied gravely. 'The children can't spell and the old woman talks too much.'

Then I talked myself for a change and she listened attentively while I told her about myself, my voyages, my books and the time of the trains from all the city stations. As she seemed so interested I told her I would meet her after school and tell her some more.

I was as good as my word. When I had eaten my lunch, instead of going on further voyages I went back to the girls' school and waited for her to come out. She seemed pleased to see me because she took my hand and brought me home with her. She lived up Gardiner's Hill, a steep, demure suburban road with trees that overhung the walls at either side. She lived in a small house on top of the hill and was one of a family of three girls. Her little brother John Joe, had been killed the previous year by a car. 'Look at what I brought home with me!' she said when we went into the kitchen, and her mother, a tall, thin woman made a great fuss of me and wanted me to have my dinner with Una. That was the girl's name. I didn't take anything, but while she ate I sat by the range and told her mother about myself as well. She seemed to like it as much as Una, and when dinner was over Una took me out in the fields behind the house for a walk.

When I went home at teatime, Mother was delighted.

'Ah,' she said, 'I knew you wouldn't be long making nice friends at school. It's about time for you, the dear knows.'

I felt much the same about it, and every fine day at three I waited for Una outside the school. When it rained and Mother would not let me out I was miserable.

One day while I was waiting for her there were two senior girls outside the gate.

'Your girl isn't out yet, Larry,' said one with a giggle.

'And do you mean to tell me Larry has a girl?' the other asked with a shocked air.

'Oh, yes,' said the first. 'Una Dwyer is Larry's girl. He goes with Una, don't you, Larry?'

I replied politely that I did, but in fact I was seriously alarmed. I had not realized that Una would be considered my girl. It had never happened to me before, and I had not understood that my waiting for her would be regarded in such a grave light. Now, I think the girls were probably right anyhow, for that is always the way it has happened to me. A woman has only to shut up and let me talk long enough for me to fall head and ears in love with her. But then I did not recognize the symptoms. All I knew was that going with somebody meant you intended to marry them. I had always planned on marrying Mother; now it seemed as if I was expected to marry someone else, and I wasn't sure if I should like it or if, like football, it would prove to be one of those games that two people could not play without pushing.

A couple of weeks later I went to a party at Una's house.

By this time it was almost as much mine as theirs. All the girls liked me and Mrs Dwyer talked to me by the hour. I saw nothing peculiar about this except a proper appreciation of geniuses. Una had warned me that I should be expected to sing, so I was ready for the occasion. I sang the Gregorian *Credo*, and some of the little girls laughed, but Mrs Dwyer only looked at me fondly.

'I suppose you'll be a priest when you grow up, Larry?' she asked.

'No, Mrs Dwyer,' I replied firmly. 'As a matter of fact, I intend to be a composer. Priests can't marry, you see, and I want to get married.'

That seemed to surprise her quite a bit. I was quite prepared to continue discussing my plans for the future, but all the children talked together. I was used to planning discussions so that they went on for a long time, but I found that whenever I began one in the Dwyers, it was immediately interrupted so that I found it hard to concentrate. Besides, all the children shouted, and Mrs Dwyer, for all her gentleness, shouted with them and at them. At first, I was somewhat alarmed, but I soon saw that they meant no particular harm, and when the party ended I was jumping up and down on the sofa, shrieking louder than anyone while Una, in hysterics of giggling, encouraged me. She seemed to think I was the funniest thing ever.

It was a moonlit November night, and lights were burning in the little cottages along the road when Una brought me home. On the road outside she stopped uncertainly and said, 'This is where little John Joe was killed.'

There was nothing remarkable about the spot, and I saw no chance of acquiring any useful information.

'Was it a Ford or a Morris?' I asked, more out of politeness than anything else.

'I don't know,' she replied with smouldering anger. 'It was Donegan's old car. They can never look where they're going, the old shows!'

'Our Lord probably wanted him,' I said perfunctorily.

'I dare say He did,' Una replied, though she showed no particular conviction. 'That old fool, Donegan – I could kill him whenever I think of it.'

'You should get your mother to make you another,' I suggested helpfully.

'Make me a what?' Una exclaimed in consternation.

'Make you another brother,' I repeated earnestly. 'It's quite easy, really. She has an engine in her tummy, and all your daddy has to do is to start it with his starting-handle.'

'Cripes!' Una said, and clapped her hand over her mouth in an explosion of giggles. 'Imagine me telling her that!'

'But it's true, Una,' I said obstinately. 'It only takes nine months. She could make you another little brother by next summer.'

'Oh, Jay!' exclaimed Una in another fit of giggles. 'Who told you all that?'

'Mummy did. Didn't your mother tell you?'

'Oh, she says you buy them from Nurse Daly,' said Una, and began to giggle again.

'I wouldn't really believe that,' I said with as much dignity as I could muster.

But the truth was I felt I had made a fool of myself again. I realized now that I had never been convinced by Mother's explanation. It was too simple. If there was anything that woman could get wrong she did so without fail. And it upset me, because for the first time I found myself wanting to make a really good impression. The Dwyers had managed to convince me that whatever else I wanted to be I did not want to be a priest. I didn't even want to be an explorer, a career which would take me away for long periods from my wife and family. I was prepared to be a composer and nothing but a composer.

That night in bed I sounded Mother on the subject of marriage. I tried to be tactful because it had always been agreed between us that I should marry her and I did not wish her to see that my feelings had changed.

'Mummy,' I asked, 'if a gentleman asks a lady to marry him, what does he say?'

'Oh,' she replied shortly, 'some of them say a lot. They say more than they mean.'

She was so irritable that I guessed she had divined my secret and I felt really sorry for her.

'If a gentleman said, "Excuse me, will you marry me?" would that be all right?' I persisted.

'Ah, well, he'd have to tell her first that he was fond of her,' said Mother who, no matter what she felt, could never bring herself to deceive me on any major issue.

But about the other matter I saw that it was hopeless to ask her any more. For days I made the most pertinacious inquiries at school and received some startling information. One boy had actually come floating down on a snowflake, wearing a bright blue dress, but to his chagrin and mine, the dress had been given away to a poor child in the North Main Street. I grieved long and deeply over this wanton destruction of evidence. The balance of opinion favoured Mrs Dwyer's solution, but of the theory of engines and starting-handles no one in the school had ever heard. That theory might have been all right when Mother was a girl but it was now definitely out of fashion.

And because of it I had been exposed to ridicule before the family whose good opinion I valued most. It was hard enough to keep up my dignity with a girl who was doing algebra while I hadn't got beyond long division without falling into childish errors that made her laugh. That is another thing I still cannot stand, being made fun of by women. Once they begin on it they never stop. Once when we were going up Gardiner's Hill together after school she stopped to look at a baby in a pram. The baby grinned at her and she gave him her finger to suck. He waved his fists and sucked like mad, and she went off into giggles again.

'I suppose that was another engine?' she said.

Four times at least she mentioned my silliness, twice in front of other girls and each time, though I pretended to ignore it, I was pierced to the heart. It made me determined not to be exposed again. Once Mother asked Una and her younger sister, Joan, to tea, and all the time I was in an agony of self-consciousness, dreading what she would say next. I felt that a woman who had said such things about babies was capable of anything. Then the talk turned on the death of little John Joe, and it all flowed back into my mind on a wave of mortification. I made two efforts to change the conversation, but Mother returned to it. She was full of pity for the Dwyers, full of sympathy for the little boy and had almost reduced herself to tears. Finally, I got up and ordered Una and Joan to play with me. Then Mother got angry.

'For goodness' sake, Larry, let the children finish their tea!' she snapped.

'It's all right, Mrs Delaney,' Una said good-naturedly. 'I'll go with him.'

'Nonsense, Una!' Mother said sharply. 'Finish your tea and go on with what you were saying. It's a wonder to me your poor mother didn't go out of her mind. How can they let people like that drive cars?'

At this I set up a loud wail. At any moment now I felt she was going to get on to babies and advise Una about what her mother ought to do.

'Will you behave yourself, Larry!' Mother said in a quivering voice. 'Or what's come over you in the past few weeks? You used to have such nice manners, and now look at you! A little corner boy! I'm ashamed of you!'

How could she know what had come over me? How could she realize that I was imagining the family circle in the Dwyers' house and Una, between fits of laughter, describing my old-fashioned mother who still talked about babies coming out of people's stomachs? It must have been real love, for I have never known true love in which I wasn't ashamed of Mother.

And she knew it and was hurt. I still enjoyed going home with

Una in the afternoons and while she ate her dinner, I sat at the piano and pretended to play my own compositions, but whenever she called at our house for me I grabbed her by the hand and tried to drag her away so that she and Mother shouldn't start talking.

'Ah, I'm disgusted with you,' Mother said one day. 'One would think you were ashamed of me in front of that little girl. I'll engage she doesn't treat her mother like that.'

Then one day I was waiting for Una at the school gate as usual. Another boy was waiting there as well – one of the seniors. When he heard the screams of the school breaking up he strolled away and stationed himself at the foot of the hill by the crossroads. Then Una herself came rushing out in her wide-brimmed felt hat, swinging her satchel, and approached me with a conspiratorial air.

'Oh, Larry, guess what's happened!' she whispered. 'I can't bring you home with me today. I'll come down and see you during the week though. Will that do?'

'Yes, thank you,' I said in a dead cold voice. Even at the most tragic moment of my life I could be nothing but polite. I watched her scamper down the hill to where the big boy was waiting. He looked over his shoulder with a grin, and then the two of them went off together.

Instead of following them I went back up the hill alone and stood leaning over the quarry wall, looking at the roadway and the valley of the city beneath me. I knew this was the end. I was too young to marry Una. I didn't know where babies came from and I didn't understand algebra. The fellow she had gone home with probably knew everything about both. I was full of gloom and revengeful thoughts. I, who had considered it sinful and dangerous to fight, was now regretting that I hadn't gone after him to batter his teeth in and jump on his face. It wouldn't even have mattered to me that I was too young and weak and that he would have done all the battering. I saw that love was a game that two people couldn't play at without pushing, just like football.

I went home and, without saying a word, took out the work

I had been neglecting so long. That too seemed to have lost its appeal. Moodily I ruled five lines and began to trace the difficult sign of the treble clef.

'Didn't you see Una, Larry?' Mother asked in surprise, looking up from her sewing.

'No, Mummy,' I said, too full for speech.

'Wisha, 'twasn't a falling-out ye had?' she asked in dismay, coming towards me. I put my head on my hands and sobbed. 'Wisha, never mind, childeen!' she murmured, running her hand through my hair. 'She was a bit old for you. You reminded her of her little brother that was killed, of course – that was why. You'll soon make new friends, take my word for it.'

But I did not believe her. That evening there was no comfort for me. My great work meant nothing to me and I knew it was all I would ever have. For all the difference it made I might as well become a priest. I felt it was a poor, sad, lonesome thing being nothing but a genius.

The Rug
EDNA O'BRIEN

I went down on my knees upon the brand-new linoleum, and smelled the strange smell. It was rich and oily. It first entered and attached itself to something in my memory when I was nine years old. I've since learned that it is the smell of linseed oil, but coming on it unexpectedly can make me both a little disturbed and sad.

I grew up in the west of Ireland, in a grey cut-stone farmhouse, which my father inherited from his father. My father came from lowland, better-off farming people, my mother from the windswept hungry hills above a great lake. As children, we played in a small forest of rhododendrons – thickened and tangled and broken under scratching cows – around the house and down the drive. The avenue up from the front gates had such great potholes that cars had to lurch off into the field and out again.

But though all outside was neglect, overgrown with rag-wort and thistle, strangers were surprised when they entered the house; my father might fritter his life away watching the slates slip from the outhouse roofs – but, within, that safe, square, lowland house of stone was my mother's pride and joy. It was always spotless. It was stuffed with things – furniture, china dogs, toby mugs, tall jugs, trays, tapestries and whatnots. Each of the four bedrooms had holy pictures on the walls and a gold overmantel surmounting each fireplace. In the fireplaces there were paper fans or lids of chocolate boxes. Mantelpieces carried their own close-packed array of wax flowers, holy statues, broken alarm clocks, shells, photographs, soft rounded cushions for sticking pins in.

My father was generous, foolish, and so idle that it could only have been some sort of illness. That year in which I was nine and first experienced the wonderful smell, he sold another of the meadows to pay off some debt, and for the first time in many years my mother got a lump of money.

She went out early one morning and caught the bus to the city, and through a summer morning and afternoon she trudged around looking at linoleums. When she came home in the evening, her feet hurting from high heels, she said she had bought some beautiful light-brown linoleum, with orange squares on it.

The day came when the four rolls were delivered to the front gates, and Hickey, our farm help, got the horse and cart ready to bring it up. We all went; we were that excited. The calves followed the cart, thinking that maybe they were to be fed down by the roadside. At times they galloped away but came back again, each calf nudging the other out of the way. It was a warm, still day, the sounds of cars and neighbours' dogs carried very distinctly and the cow pats on the drive were brown and dry like flake tobacco.

My mother did most of the heaving and shoving to get the rolls on to the cart. She had early accepted that she had been born to do the work.

She may have bribed Hickey with the promise of hens to sell for himself, because that evening he stayed in to help with the floor – he usually went over to the village and drank a pint or two of stout. Mama, of course, always saved newspapers, and she said that the more we laid down under the lino the longer it would wear. On her hands and knees, she looked up once – flushed, delighted, tired – and said, 'Mark my words, we'll see a carpet in here yet.'

There was calculation and argument before cutting the difficult bits around the door frames, the bay window, and the fireplace. Hickey said that without him my mother would have botched the whole thing. In the quick flow of argument and talk, they did not notice that it was past my bedtime. My father sat outside in the kitchen by the stove all evening while we worked. Later, he came in and said what a grand job we were doing. A grand job, he said. He'd had a headache.

The next day must have been Saturday, for I sat in the sitting-room all morning admiring the linoleum, smelling its smell, counting the orange squares. I was supposed to be dusting. Now and then I rearranged the blinds, as the sun moved. We had to keep the sun from fading the bright colours.

The dogs barked and the postman cycled up. I ran out and met him carrying a huge parcel. Mama was away up in the yard with the hens. When the postman had gone, I went up to tell her.

'A parcel?' she said. She was cleaning the hens' trough before putting their food in it. The hens were moiling around, falling in and out of the buckets, pecking at her hands. 'It's just binding twine for the bailing machine,' she said. 'Who'd be sending parcels?' She was never one to lose her head.

I said that the parcel had a Dublin postmark – the postman told me that – and that there was some black woolly thing in it. The paper was torn at the corner, and I'd pushed a finger in, fearfully.

Coming down to the house she wiped her hands with a wad of long grass. 'Perhaps somebody in America has remembered us at last.' One of her few dreams was to be remembered by relatives who had gone to America. The farm buildings were some way from the house; we ran the last bit. But, even in her excitement, her careful nature forced her to unknot every length of string from the parcel and roll it up, for future use. She was the world's most generous woman, but was thrifty about saving twine and paper, and candle stumps, and turkey wings and empty pill boxes.

'My God,' she said reverently, folding back the last piece of paper and revealing a black sheepskin hearth-rug. We opened it out. It was a half-moon shape and covered the kitchen table. She could not speak. It was real sheepskin, thick and soft and luxurious. She examined the lining, studied the maker's label in the back, searched through the folds of brown paper for a possible letter, but there was nothing at all to indicate where it had come from.

'Get me my glasses,' she said. We read the address again, and the postmark. The parcel had been sent from Dublin two days before. 'Call your father,' she said. He was in bed with rheumatic pains. Rug or no rug, he demanded a fourth cup of tea before he could get up.

We carried the big black rug into the sitting-room and laid it down upon the new linoleum, before the fireplace.

'Isn't it perfect, a perfect colour scheme?' she said. The room had suddenly become cosy. She stood back and looked at it with surprise, and a touch of suspicion. Though she was always hoping, she never really expected things to turn out well. At nine years old, I knew enough about my mother's life to say a prayer of thanks that at last she had got something she wanted, and without having to work for it. She had a round, sallow face and a peculiarly uncertain, timid smile. The suspicion soon left her, and the smile came out. That was one of her happiest days; I remember it as I remember her unhappiest day to my knowledge – the day the bailiff came, a year later. I hoped she would sit in the newly appointed room on Sundays for tea, without her apron, with her brown hair combed out, looking calm and beautiful. Outside, the rhododendrons, though wild and broken, would bloom red and purple and, inside, the new rug would lie upon the richly smelling linoleum. She hugged me suddenly, as if I were the one to thank for it all; the hen mash had dried on her hands and they had the mealy smell I knew so well.

For spells during the next few days, my mother racked her brain, and she racked our brains, for a clue. It had to be someone who knew something of her needs and wants – how else could he have decided upon just the thing she needed? She wrote letters here and there, to distant relations, to friends, to people she had not seen for years.

'Must be one of *your* friends,' she would say to my father.

'Oh, probably, probably. I've known a lot of decent people in my time.'

She was referring – ironically, of course – to the many strangers to whom he had offered tea. He liked nothing better than to stand down at the gates on a fair day or a race day, engaging passers-by in conversation and finally bringing someone up to the house for tea and boiled eggs. He had a genius for making friends.

'I'd say that's it,' my father said, delighted to take credit for the rug.

In the warm evenings we sat around the fireplace – we'd never had a fire in that room throughout the whole of my childhood – and around the rug, listening to the radio. And now and then, Mama or Dada would remember someone else from whom the rug might have come. Before a week had passed, she had written to a dozen people – an acquaintance who had moved up to Dublin with a greyhound pup Dada had given him, which greyhound had turned out a winner; an unfrocked priest who had stayed in our house for a week, gathering strength from Mama to travel on home and meet his family; a magician who had stolen Dada's gold watch and never been seen since; a farmer who once sold us a tubercular cow and would not take it back.

Weeks passed. The rug was taken out on Saturdays and shaken well, the new lino polished. Once, coming home early from school, I looked in the window and saw Mama kneeling on the rug saying a prayer. I'd never seen her pray like that, in the middle of the day, before. My father was going into the next county the following day to look at a horse he thought he might get cheap; she was, of course, praying that he would keep his promise and not touch a drink. If he did, he might be off on a wild progress and would not be seen for a week.

He went the next day; he was to stay overnight with relations. While he was away, I slept with Mama, for company, in the big brass bed. I wakened to see a candle flame, and Mama hurriedly putting on her cardigan. Dada had come home? No, she said, but she had been lying awake thinking, and there was something she had to tell Hickey or she would not get a wink of sleep. It was not yet twelve; he might be awake. I didn't want to be left in the dark, I said, but she was already hurrying along the landing. I nipped out of bed, and followed. The luminous clock said a quarter to twelve. From the first landing, I looked over and saw her turning the knob of Hickey's door.

Why should he open his door to her then? I thought; he never let anyone in at any time, keeping the door locked when he was out on the farm. Once we climbed in through the window and found things in such a muddle – his good suit laid out flat on the floor, a shirt soaking in a bucket of dirty green water, a milk can in which there was curdled buttermilk, a bicycle chain, a broken Sacred Heart and several pairs of worn, distorted, cast-off boots – that she resolved never to set foot in it again.

'What the hell is it?' Hickey said. Then there was a thud. He must have knocked something over while he searched for his flashlamp.

'If it's fine tomorrow, we'll cut the turf,' Mama said.

Hickey asked if she'd wakened him at that hour to tell him something he already knew – they discussed it at tea-time.

'Open the door,' she said. 'I have a bit of news for you, about the rug.'

He opened the door just a fraction. 'Who sent it?' he asked.

'That party from Ballinsloe,' she said.

'That party' was her phrase for her two visitors who had come to our house years before – a young girl, and an older man who wore brown gauntlet gloves. Almost as soon as they'd arrived, my father went out with them in their motor car. When they returned to our house an hour later, I gathered from the conversation that they had been to see our local doctor, a friend of Dad's. The girl was the sister of a nun, who was headmistress at the convent where my sisters were. She had been crying. I guessed then, or maybe later, that her tears had to do with her having a baby and that Dada had taken her to the doctor so that she could find out for certain if she were pregnant and make preparations to get married. It would have been impossible for her to go to a doctor in her own neighbourhood, and I had no doubt but that Dada was glad to do a favour for the nun, as he could not always pay the fees for my sisters' education. Mama gave them tea on a tray – not a spread with hand-embroidered cloth and bone-china cups – and shook hands with them coolly when they were leaving. She could not abide sinful people.

'Nice of them to remember,' Hickey said, sucking air between his teeth and making bird noises. 'How did you find out?'

'I just guessed,' Mama told him.

'Oh, Christ!' Hickey said, closing his door with a fearful bang and getting back into bed with such vehemence that I could hear the springs revolt.

Mama carried me up the stairs, because my feet were cold, and said that Hickey had not one ounce of manners.

Next day, when Dad came home sober, she told him the story, and that night she wrote to the nun. In due course, a letter came to us – with holy medals and scapulars enclosed for me – saying that neither the nun nor her married sister had sent a gift. I expect the girl had married the man with the gauntlet gloves.

''Twill be one of life's mysteries,' Mama said, as she beat the rug against the pier, closed her eyes to escape the dust and reconciled herself to never knowing.

But a knock came on our back door four weeks later, when we were upstairs changing the sheets on the beds. 'Run down and see who it is,' she said.

It was a namesake of Dada's from the village, a man who always came to borrow something – a donkey, or a mowing machine, or even a spade.

'Is your mother in?' he asked, and I went half-way up the stairs and called her down.

'I've come for the rug,' he said.

'What rug?' Mama asked. It was the nearest she ever got to lying. Her breath caught short and she blushed a little.

'I hear you have a new rug here. Well, 'tis our rug, because my wife's sister sent it to us months ago and we never got it.'

'What are you talking about?' she said in a very sarcastic voice. He was a cowardly man, and it was said that he was so ineffectual he would call his wife in from the garden to pour him a cup of tea. I suppose my mother hoped that she would frighten him off.

'The rug the postman brought here one morning, and handed it to your youngster there.' He nodded at me.

'Oh, that,' Mama said, a little stunned by the news that the postman had given information about it. Then a ray of hope, or a ray of lunacy, must have struck her, because she asked what colour of rug he was inquiring about.

'A black sheepskin,' he said.

There could be no more doubt about it. Her whole being drooped – shoulders, stomach, voice, everything.

'It's here,' she said absently, and she went through the hall into the sitting-room.

'Being namesakes and that, the postman got us mixed up,' he said stupidly to me.

She had winked at me to stay there and see he did not follow her, because she did not want him to know that we had been using it.

It was rolled and had a piece of cord around the middle when she handed it to him. As she watched him go down the avenue she wept, not so much for the loss – though the loss was enormous – as for her own foolishness in thinking that someone had wanted to do her a kindness at last.

'We live and learn,' she said, as she undid her apron strings, out of habit, and then retied them slowly and methodically, making a tighter knot.

The Exercise

BERNARD MacLAVERTY

'We never got the chance,' his mother would say to him. 'It wouldn't have done me much good but your father could have bettered himself. He'd be teaching or something now instead of serving behind a bar. He could stand up with the best of them.'

Now that he had started grammar school Kevin's father joined him in his work, helping him when he had the time, sometimes doing the exercises out of the text books on his own before he went to bed. He worked mainly from examples in the Maths and Language books or from previously corrected work of Kevin's. Often his wife took a hand out of him, saying 'Do you think you'll pass your Christmas Tests?'

When he concentrated he sat hunched at the kitchen table, his non-writing hand shoved down the back of his trousers and his tongue stuck out.

'Put that thing back in your mouth,' Kevin's mother would say, laughing. 'You've a tongue on you like a cow.'

His father smelt strongly of tobacco for he smoked both a pipe and cigarettes. When he gave Kevin money for sweets he'd say, 'You'll get sixpence in my coat pocket on the banisters.'

Kevin would dig into the pocket deep down almost to his elbow and pull out a handful of coins speckled with bits of yellow and black tobacco. His father also smelt of porter, not his breath, for he never drank but from his clothes and Kevin thought it mixed nicely with his grown-up smell. He loved to smell his pyjama jacket and the shirts that he left off for washing.

Once in a while Kevin's father would come in at six o'clock, sit in his armchair and say, 'Slippers.'

'You're not staying in, are you?' The three boys shouted and danced around, the youngest pulling off his big boots, falling back on the floor as they came away from his feet, Kevin, the eldest, standing on the arm of the chair to get the slippers down from the cupboard.

'Some one of you get a good shovel of coal for that fire,' and they sat in the warm kitchen doing their homework, their father reading the paper or moving about doing some job that their mother had been at him to do for months. Before their bedtime he would read the younger ones a story or if there were no books in the house at the time he would choose a piece from the paper. Kevin listened with the others although he pretended to be doing something else.

But it was not one of those nights. His father stood shaving with his overcoat on, a very heavy navy overcoat, in a great hurry, his face creamed thick with white lather. Kevin knelt on the cold lino of the bathroom floor, one elbow leaning on the padded seat of the green wicker chair trying to get help with his Latin. It was one of those exercises which asked for the nominative and genitive of: an evil deed, a wise father and so on.

'What's the Latin for "evil"?'

His father towered above him trying to get at the mirror, pointing his chin upwards scraping underneath.

'Look it up at the back.'

Kevin sucked the end of his pencil and fumbled through the vocabularies. His father finished shaving, humped his back and spluttered in the basin. Kevin heard him pull the plug and the final gasp as the water escaped. He groped for the towel then genuflected beside him drying his face.

'Where is it?' He looked down still drying slower and slower, meditatively until he stopped.

'I'll tell you just this once because I'm in a hurry.'

Kevin stopped sucking the pencil and held it poised ready, and wrote the answers with great speed into his jotter as his father called them out.

'Is that them all?' his father asked, draping the towel over the side of the bath. He leaned forward to kiss Kevin but he lowered his head to look at something in the book. As he rushed down the stairs he shouted back over his shoulder.

'Don't ever ask me to do that again. You'll have to work them out for yourself.'

He was away leaving Kevin sitting at the chair. The towel edged its way slowly down the side of the bath and fell on the floor. He got up and looked in the wash-hand basin. The bottom was covered in short black hairs, shavings. He drew a white path through them with his finger. Then he turned and went down the stairs to copy the answers in ink.

Of all the teachers in the school Waldo was the one who commanded the most respect. In his presence nobody talked, with the result that he walked the corridors in a moat of silence. Boys seeing him approach would drop their voices to a whisper and only when he was out of earshot would they speak normally again. Between classes there was always five minutes' uproar. The boys wrestled over desks, shouted, whistled, flung books while some tried to learn their verbs, eyes closed, feet tapping to the rhythm of declensions. Others put frantic finishing touches to last night's exercise. Some minutes before

Waldo's punctual arrival, the class quietened. Three rows of boys, all by now strumming verbs, sat hunched and waiting.

Waldo's entrance was theatrical. He strode in with strides as long as his soutane would permit, his books clenched in his left hand and pressed tightly against his chest. With his right hand he swung the door behind him, closing it with a crash. His eyes raked the class. If, as occasionally happened, it did not close properly he did not turn from the class but backed slowly against the door snapping it shut with his behind. Two strides brought him to the rostrum. He cracked his books down with an explosion and made a swift palm upward gesture.

Waldo was very tall, his height being emphasized by the soutane, narrow and tight-fitting at the shoulders, sweeping down like a bell to the floor. A row of black gleaming buttons bisected him from floor to throat. When he talked his Adam's apple hit against the hard, white Roman collar and created in Kevin the same sensation as a fingernail scraping down the blackboard. His face was sallow and immobile. (There was a rumour that he had a glass eye but no one knew which. Nobody could look at him long enough because to meet his stare was to invite a question.) He abhorred slovenliness. Once when presented with an untidy exercise book, dog-eared with a tea ring on the cover, he picked it up, the corner of one leaf between his finger and thumb, the pages splaying out like a fan, opened the window and dropped it three floors to the ground. His own neatness became exaggerated when he was at the board, writing in copperplate script just large enough for the boy in the back row to read – geometrical columns of declined verbs defined by exact, invisible margins. When he had finished he would set the chalk down and rub the used finger and thumb together with the same action he used after handling the host over the paten.

The palm upward gesture brought the class to its feet and they said the Hail Mary in Latin. While it was being said all eyes looked down because they knew if they looked up Waldo was bound to be staring at them.

'Exercises.'

When Waldo was in a hurry he corrected the exercises verbally, asking one boy for the answers and then asking all those who got it right to put up their hands. It was four for anyone who lied about his answer and now and then he would take spot checks to find out the liars.

'Hold it, hold it there,' he would say and leap from the rostrum, moving through the forest of hands and look at each boy's book, tracing out the answer with the tip of his cane. Before the end of the round and while his attention was on one book a few hands would be lowered quietly. Today he was in a hurry. The atmosphere was tense as he looked from one boy to another, deciding who would start.

'Sweeny, we'll begin with you.' Kevin rose to his feet, his finger trembling under the place in the book. He read the first answer and looked up at Waldo. He remained impassive. He would let someone while translating unseens ramble on and on with great imagination until he faltered, stopped and admitted that he didn't know. Then and only then would he be slapped.

'Two, nominative. *Sapienter Pater*.' Kevin went on haltingly through the whole ten and stopped, waiting for a comment from Waldo. It was a long time before he spoke. When he did it was with bored annoyance.

'Every last one of them is wrong.'

'But sir, Father, they couldn't be wr–', Kevin said it with such conviction, blurted it out so quickly that Waldo looked at him in surprise.

'Why not?'

'Because my . . .' Kevin stopped.

'Well?' Waldo's stone face resting on his knuckles. 'Because my what?'

It was too late to turn back now.

'Because my father said so,' he mumbled very low, chin on chest.

'Speak up, let us all hear you.' Some of the boys had heard and he thought they sniggered.

'Because my father said so.' This time the commotion in the class was obvious.

'And where does your father teach Latin?' There was no escape. Waldo had him. He knew now there would be an exhibition for the class. Kevin placed his weight on his arm and felt his tremble communicated to the desk.

'He doesn't, Father.'

'And what does he do?'

Kevin hesitated, stammering,

'He's a barman.'

'A barman!' Waldo mimicked and the class roared loudly.

'*Quiet.*' He wheeled on them. 'You, Sweeny. Come out here.' He reached inside the breast of his soutane and with a flourish produced a thin yellow cane, whipping it back and forth, testing it.

Kevin walked out to the front of the class, his face fiery red, the blood throbbing in his ears. He held out his hand. Waldo raised it higher, more to his liking, with the tip of the cane touching the underside of the upturned palm. He held it there for some time.

'If your brilliant father continues to do your homework for you, Sweeny, you'll end up a barman yourself.' Then he whipped the cane down expertly across the tips of his fingers and again just as the blood began to surge back into them. Each time the cane in its follow-through cracked loudly against the skirts of his soutane.

'You could have made a better job of it yourself. Other hand.' The same ritual of raising and lowering the left hand with the tip of the cane to the desired height. 'After all, I have taught you some Latin.' *Crack*. 'It would be hard to do any worse.'

Kevin went back to his place resisting a desire to hug his hands under his armpits and stumbled on a schoolbag jutting into the aisle as he pushed into his desk. Again Waldo looked round the class and said, 'Now we'll have it *right* from someone.'

The class continued and Kevin nursed his fingers, out of the fray.

As the bell rang Waldo gathered up his books and said, 'Sweeny, I want a word with you outside. *Ave Maria, gratia plena . . .*' It was not until the end of the corridor that Waldo turned to face him. He looked at Kevin and maintained his silence for a moment.

'Sweeny, I must apologize to you.' Kevin bowed his head. 'I meant your father no harm – he's probably a good man, a very good man.'

'Yes, sir,' said Kevin. The pain in his fingers had gone.

'Look at me when I'm talking, please.' Kevin looked at his collar, his Adam's apple, then his face. It relaxed for a fraction and Kevin thought he was almost going to smile, but he became efficient, abrupt again.

'All right, very good, you may go back to your class.'

'Yes Father,' Kevin nodded and moved back along the empty corridor.

Some nights when he had finished his homework early he would go down to meet his father coming home from work. It was dark, October, and he stood close against the high wall at the bus-stop trying to shelter from the cutting wind. His thin black blazer with the school emblem on the breast pocket and his short grey trousers, both new for starting grammar school, did little to keep him warm. He stood shivering, his hands in his trouser pockets and looked down at his knees which were blue and marbled, quivering uncontrollably. It was six o'clock when he left the house and he had been standing for fifteen minutes. Traffic began to thin out and the buses became less regular, carrying fewer and fewer passengers. There was a moment of silence when there was no traffic and he heard a piece of paper scraping along on pointed edges. He kicked it as it passed him. He thought of what had happened, of Waldo and his father. On the first day in class Waldo had picked out many boys by their names.

'Yes, I know your father well,' or 'I taught your elder brother. A fine priest he's made. Next.'

'Sweeny, Father.'

'Sweeny? Sweeny? – You're not Dr John's son, are you?'

'No Father.'

'Or anything to do with the milk people?'

'No Father.'

'Next.' He passed on without further comment.

Twenty-five past six. Another bus turned the corner and Kevin saw his father standing on the platform. He moved forward to the stop as the bus slowed down. His father jumped lightly off and saw Kevin waiting for him. He clipped him over the head with the tightly rolled newspaper he was carrying.

'How are you big lad?'

'All right,' said Kevin shivering. He humped his shoulders and set off beside his father, bumping into him uncertainly as he walked.

'How did it go today?' his father asked.

'All right.' They kept silent until they reached the corner of their own street.

'What about the Latin?'

Kevin faltered, feeling a babyish desire to cry.

'How was it?'

'OK. Fine.'

'Good. I was a bit worried about it. It was done in a bit of a rush. Son, your Da's a genius.' He smacked him with the paper again. Kevin laughed and slipped his hand into the warmth of his father's overcoat pocket, deep to the elbow.

The Confirmation Suit

BRENDAN BEHAN

For weeks it was nothing but simony and sacrilege, and the sins crying to heaven for vengeance, the big green Catechism in our hands, walking home along the North Circular Road. And after tea, at the back of the brewery wall, with a butt too to help our wits, what is a pure spirit, and don't kill that, Billser has to get a drag out of it yet, what do I mean by apostate, and hell and heaven and despair and presumption and hope. The big fellows, who were now thirteen and the veterans of last year's Confirmation, frightened us, and said the Bishop would fire us out of the Chapel if we didn't answer his questions, and we'd be left wandering around the streets, in a new suit and top-coat with nothing to show for it, all dressed up and nowhere to go. The big people said not to mind them; they were only getting it up for us, jealous because they were over their Confirmation, and could never make it again. At school we were in a special room to ourselves, for the last few days, and went round, a special class of people. There were worrying times too, that the Bishop would light on you, and you wouldn't be able to answer his questions. Or you might hear the women complaining about the price of boys' clothes.

'Twenty-two and sixpence for tweed, I'd expect a share in the shop for that. I've a good mind to let him go in jersey and pants for that.'

'Quite right, ma'am,' says one to another, backing one another up, 'I always say what matter if they are good and pure.' What had that got to do with it, if you had to go into the Chapel in a jersey and pants, and every other kid in a new suit, kid gloves and tan shoes and a scoil cap. The Cowan brothers were terrified. They were twins, and twelve years old, and every old one in the street seemed to be wishing a jersey and pants on them, and saying their poor mother couldn't be expected to do for two in the one year, and she ought to go down to Sister Monica and tell her to put one back. If it came to that, the Cowans agreed to fight it out, at the back of the brewery wall; whoever got best, the other would be put back.

I wasn't so worried about this. My old fellow was a tradesman, and made money most of the time. Besides, my grandmother, who lived at the top of the next house, was a lady of capernoity and function. She had money and lay in bed all day, drinking porter or malt, and taking pinches of snuff, and talking to the neighbours that would call up to tell her the news of the day. She only left her bed to go down one flight of stairs and visit the lady in the back drawing room, Miss McCann.

Miss McCann worked a sewing-machine, making habits for the dead. Sometimes girls from our quarter got her to make dresses and costumes, but mostly she stuck to the habits. They were a steady line, she said, and you didn't have to be always buying patterns, for the fashions didn't change, not even from summer to winter. They were like a long brown shirt, and a hood attached, that was closed over the person's face before the coffin lid was screwn down. A sort of little banner hung out of one arm, made of the same material, and four silk rosettes in each corner, and in the middle, the letters I.H.S., which mean, Miss McCann said, 'I Have Suffered'.

My grandmother and Miss McCann liked me more than any other kid they knew. I like being liked, and could only admire their taste.

My Aunt Jack, who was my father's aunt as well as mine, sometimes came down from where she lived, up near the Basin, where the water came from before they started getting it from Wicklow. My Aunt Jack said it was much better water, at that. Miss McCann said she ought to be a good judge. For Aunt Jack was funny. She didn't drink porter or malt, or take snuff, and my father said she never thought much about men either. She was also very strict about washing yourself very often. My grandmother took a bath every year, whether she was dirty or not, but she was in no way bigoted in the washing line in between times.

Aunt Jack made terrible raids on us now and again, to stop snuff and drink, and make my grandmother get up in the morning, and wash herself, and cook meals and take food with them. My grandmother was a gilder by trade, and served her time in one of the best shops in the city, and was getting a man's wages at sixteen. She liked stuff out of the pork butchers, and out of cans, but didn't like boiling potatoes, for she said she was no skivvy, and the chip man was better at it. When she was left alone it was a pleasure to eat with her. She always had cans of lovely things and spicy meat and brawn, and plenty of seasoning, fresh out of the German man's shop up the road. But after a visit from Aunt Jack, she would have to get up and wash for a week, and she would have to go and make stews and boil cabbage and pig's cheeks. Aunt Jack was very much up for sheep's heads too. They were so cheap and nourishing.

But my grandmother only tried it once. She had been a first-class gilder in Eustace Street, but never had anything to do with sheep's heads before. When she took it out of the pot, and laid it on the plate, she and I sat looking at it, in fear and trembling. It was bad enough going into the pot, but with the soup streaming from its eyes, and its big teeth clenched in a very bad temper, it would put the heart crossways in you. My grandmother asked me, in a whisper, if I ever thought sheep could look so vindictive, but that it was more like the head of an old man, and would I for God's sake take it up and throw it out of the window. The sheep kept glaring at us, but I came the far side of it, and rushed over to the window and threw it out in a flash. My grandmother had to drink a Baby Power whiskey, for she wasn't the better of herself.

Afterwards she kept what she called her stock-pot on the gas. A heap of bones and, as she said herself, any old muck that would come in handy, to have boiling there, night and day, on a glimmer. She and I ate happily of cooked ham and California pineapple and sock-eyed salmon, and the pot of good nourishing soup was always on the gas even if Aunt Jack came down the chimney, like the Holy Souls at midnight. My grandmother said she didn't begrudge the money for the gas. Not when she remembered the looks that sheep's head was giving her. And all she had to do with the stock-pot was throw in another sup of water, now and again, and a handful of old rubbish the pork butcher would send over, in the way of lights or bones. My Aunt Jack thought a lot about barley, too, so we had a package of that lying beside the gas, and threw a sprinkle in any time her foot was heard on the stairs. The stock-pot bubbled away on the gas for years after, and only when my grandmother was dead did someone notice it. They tasted it, and spat it out just as quick, and wondered what it was. Some said it was paste, and more that it was gold size, and there were other people and they maintained that it was glue. They all agreed to one thing, that it was dangerous tack to leave lying around where there might be young children, and in the heel of the reel, it went out the same window as the sheep's head.

Miss McCann told my grandmother not to mind Aunt Jack but to sleep as long as she liked in the morning. They came to an arrangement that Miss McCann would cover the landing and keep an eye out. She would call Aunt Jack in for a minute, and give the signal by banging the grate, letting on to poke the fire, and have a bit of a conversation with Aunt Jack about dresses and costumes, and hats and habits. One of these mornings, and Miss McCann delaying a fighting action, to give my grandmother time to hurl herself out of bed and into her clothes and give her face a rub of a towel, the chat between Miss McCann and Aunt Jack came to my Confirmation suit.

When I made my first Communion, my grandmother dug deep under the mattress, and myself and Aunt Jack were sent round expensive shops, and I came back with a rig that would take the sight of your eye. This time, however, Miss McCann said there wasn't much stirring in the habit line, on account of the mild winter, and she would be delighted to make the suit, if Aunt Jack would get the material. I nearly wept, for terror of what these old women would have me got up in, but I had to let on to be delighted, Miss McCann was so set on it. She asked Aunt Jack did she remember my father's Confirmation suit. *He* did. He said he would never forget it. They sent him out in a velvet suit, of plum colour, with a lace collar. My blood ran cold when he told me.

The stuff they got for my suit was blue serge, and that was not so bad. They got as far as the pants, and that passed off very civil. You can't do much to a boy's pants, one pair is like the next, though I had to ask them not to trouble themselves putting three little buttons on either side of the legs. The waistcoat was all right, and anyway the coat would cover it. But the coat itself, that was where Aughrim was lost.

The lapels were little wee things, like what you'd see in pictures like *Ring* magazine of John L. Sullivan, or Gentleman

Jim, and the buttons were the size of saucers, or within the bawl of an ass of it, and I nearly cried when I saw them being put on, and ran down to my mother, and begged her to get me any sort of a suit, even a jersey and pants, than have me set up before the people in this get-up. My mother said it was very kind of Aunt Jack and Miss McCann to go to all this trouble and expense, and I was very ungrateful not to appreciate it. My father said that Miss McCann was such a good tailor that people were dying to get into her creations, and her handiwork was to be found in all the best cemeteries. He laughed himself sick at this, and said if it was good enough for him to be sent down to North William Street in plum-coloured velvet and lace, I needn't be getting the needle over a couple of big buttons and little lapels. He asked me not to forget to get up early the morning of my Confirmation, and let him see me, before he went to work: a bit of a laugh started the day well. My mother told him to give over and let me alone, and said she was sure it would be a lovely suit, and that Aunt Jack would never buy poor material, but stuff that would last for ever. That nearly finished me altogether, and I ran through the hall up to the corner, fit to cry my eyes out, only I wasn't much of a hand at crying. I went more for cursing, and I cursed all belonging to me, and was hard at it on my father, and wondering why his lace collar hadn't choked him, when I remembered that it was a sin to go on like that, and I going up for Confirmation, and I had to simmer down, and live in fear of the day I'd put on that jacket.

The days passed, and I was fitted and refitted, and every old one in the house came up to look at the suit, and took a pinch of snuff, and a sup out of the jug, and wished me long life and the health to wear and tear it, and they spent that much time viewing it round, back, belly and sides, that Miss McCann hadn't time to make the overcoat, and like an answer to a prayer, I was brought down to Talbot Street, and dressed out in a dinging overcoat, belted, like a grown-up man's. And my shoes and gloves were dear and dandy, and I said to myself that there was no need to let anyone see the suit with its little lapels and big buttons. I could keep the topcoat on all day, in the chapel and going round afterwards.

The night before Confirmation day, Miss McCann handed over the suit to my mother, and kissed me, and said not to bother thanking her. She would do more than that for me, and she and my grandmother cried and had a drink on the strength of my having grown to be a big fellow, in the space of twelve years, which they didn't seem to consider a great deal of time. My father said to my mother, and I getting bathed before the fire, that since I was born Miss McCann thought the world of me. When my mother was in hospital, she took me into her place till my mother came out, and it near broke her heart to give me back.

In the morning I got up, and Mrs Rooney in the next room shouted in to my mother that her Liam was still stalling, and not making any move to get out of it, and she thought she was cursed; Christmas or Easter, Communion or Confirmation, it would drive a body into Riddleys, which is the mad part of Grangegorman, and she wondered she wasn't driven out of her mind, and above in the puzzle factory years ago. So she shouted again at Liam to get up and washed and dressed. And my mother shouted at me, though I was already knotting my tie, but you might as well be out of the world as out of fashion, and they kept it up like a pair of mad women, until at last Liam and I were ready and he came in to show my mother his clothes. She handselled him a tanner which he put in his pocket and Mrs Rooney called me in to show her my clothes. I just stood at her door, and didn't open my coat, but just grabbed the sixpence out of her hand, and ran up the stairs like the hammers of hell. She shouted at me to hold on a minute, she hadn't seen my suit, but I muttered something about it not being lucky to keep a Bishop waiting, and ran on.

The Church was crowded, boys on one side and the girls on the other, and the altar ablaze with lights and flowers, and a throne for the Bishop to sit on when he wasn't confirming.

There was a cheering crowd outside, drums rolled, trumpeters from Jim Larkin's band sounded the Salute. The Bishop came in and the doors were shut. In short order I joined the queue to the rails, knelt and was whispered over, and touched on the cheek. I had my overcoat on the whole time, though it was warm, and I was in a lather of sweat waiting for the hymns and the sermon.

The lights grew brighter and I got warmer, was carried out fainting. But though I didn't mind them loosening my tie, I clenched firmly my overcoat, and nobody saw the jacket with the big buttons and the little lapels. When I went home I got into bed, and my father said I went into a sickness just as the Bishop was giving us the pledge. He said this was a master stroke and showed real presence of mind.

Sunday after Sunday, my mother fought over the suit. She said I was a liar and a hypocrite, putting it on for a few minutes every week, and running into Miss McCann's and out again, letting her think I wore it every weekend. In a passionate temper my mother said she would show me up, and tell Miss McCann, and up like a shot with her, for my mother was always slim and light on her feet as a feather, and in next door. When she came back she said nothing, but sat at the fire looking into it. I didn't really believe she would tell Miss McCann. And I put on the suit and thought I would go in and tell her I was wearing it this week-night, because I was going to the Queen's with my brothers. I ran next door and upstairs, and every step was more certain and easy that my mother hadn't told her. I ran, shoved in the door, saying: 'Miss Mc., Miss Mc., Rory and Sean and I are going to the Queen's . . .' She was bent over the sewing-machine and all I could see was the top of her old grey head, and the rest of her shaking with crying, and her arms folded under her head, on a bit of habit where she had been finishing the I.H.S. I ran down the stairs and back into our place, and my mother was sitting at the fire, sad and sorry, but saying nothing.

I needn't have worried about the suit lasting for ever. Miss

McCann didn't. The next winter was not so mild, and she was whipped before the year was out. At her wake people said how she was in a habit of her own making, and my father said she would look queer in anything else, seeing as she supplied the dead of the whole quarter for forty years, without one complaint from a customer.

At the funeral, I left my topcoat in the carriage and got out and walked in the spills of rain after her coffin. People said I would get my end, but I went on till we reached the graveside, and I stood in my Confirmation suit drenched to the skin. I thought this was the least I could do.

from *Holy Pictures*
CLARE BOYLAN

The following day during lunch father told the family he had an announcement to make. They were glad of the diversion. Nellie was off because it was Sunday and mother had cooked a sheep's head on father's instructions. She boiled it up with an onion and brought it to the table in a serving dish. Bubbles came from the eye sockets and tufts of grey flesh bobbed on the disembodied skull. There was a sirloin of beef to follow but everyone's appetite had been affected.

He told them he had changed his name. Nan could not remember what his name was. She never heard him called anything except father. 'Cecil!' mother protested in fright. Cecil. She could understand.

He had progressed to the syrup pudding. His head was sideways, like Bertie with a bone. He was concentrating. Every few seconds he dabbed at his mouth with a napkin. 'I have decided upon Webster,' he said when his mouth was clear. 'It is a respectable name.'

'*Webster*!' Their confusion gave the name a special emphasis, as if it had to do with ducks' feet or the homes of spiders. It was not the name of a saint.

He laid down his spoon and placed his hands on the table. 'Cecil Webster.'

She saw it then, the power in those haughty hands. He had taken away their name. It was as if their lives were empty frames of his making within which he had chalked the features. He had taken a duster and wiped them clean. She glanced at her mother and saw, as she expected, a face scrubbed of all expression. Only her eyebrows rose with shock. 'Mother,' she demanded. 'He's trying to change our name.' 'Our name. Yes.' Mother made an effort to sit to attention. There was a look of mild reproach on her face. She hated being made to face things.

Her heart began to beat painfully. Nan Cantwell, Hallinan's Mansions. Nan Cantwell, Hallinan's Mansions. 'What about school?' she said cautiously. 'All the people we know.'

'Your mother will give you a note for the nuns,' he said. 'The matter scarcely concerns you. Children are not entitled to a full address. You will be known, as usual, by your Christian name.' 'Mary!' She tried to involve her sister but Mary was using her spoon to make a syrupy hill in her dish. She was smiling. Nan had to tackle father alone. 'You can't do it,' she said. 'It's our name. It's *ours*!' 'It is already done,' he said. 'Our name has been changed by deed poll.' She had never seen him so calm. 'It was necessary to do it. That is all you need to know. Names do not matter to women. They are only of interest to peopie in the world. Women do not have a name until they marry.'

She could not argue with him. He was too powerful. He was a storm, blowing them this way and that, shaking loose their hold on ordinary things. He was the one who had ordered their mundane existence, refusing to send the girls to a good school because only boys required an education. It was not that Nan wanted ordinary things. She wanted the extraordinary but when it happened she had still to be enough herself to experience it.

'Why?' she begged.

There was an odd wistful look on father's face as if he was actually considering the question and then he remembered it was a child, giving cheek. 'Because I have said it,' he barked.

The edges of her jaws were clutched by numbness. It was a warning of tears. She folded her napkin carefully and put it on the table. 'The one meal of the week we eat together and she has to cause a barney,' she heard father's voice complain. She kept her head down when she pushed back her chair and ran out into the street. She felt as if she had been slapped. It was the unfairness that stung. 'Women do not have a name until they marry!' Mother was married and he was taking away her name. Why couldn't they leave him? Why couldn't they find a place to live on their own in peace? Nellie managed. She knew the answer. Mother liked being married. She liked not having to work or to worry about money. Although she was afraid of father, she was proud of him. He gave her stature with the neighbours. There were details of marriage that disturbed her but she liked being Mrs Cantwell. Oh, mother, Nan thought. How will you face your neighbours without your name? It was her only vanity.

Running along the warm pavement, her head ducked, Nan made up her mind that she would never go back. 'I shall run away. I shall make my own way in the world.' She had a vague, exciting picture of boats and restaurants, a group of working girls with sweaters, one of them with her face. There intruded on this an image of mother peering uneasily into a saucepan while water gushed menacingly from the tap. She would have turned there and then and raced back to her had it not been for another disturbance to her thoughts.

'Hello.'

She looked up. 'Dandy!'

'Walk?' Dandy's hair fell across her face and she slouched in an indifferent fashion.

Nan had not intended to talk to her ever again but she had to talk to someone and mother had said she must not see the Jews. Dandy knew about life. She would know if it was normal for the curse to go on for a second day. She would have something to say about fathers who gave and took names as they pleased. 'Where will we go?' she said.

Dandy thought. 'We could go to the morgue.'

They walked in silence. Once Dandy stopped to say, 'I saw you from the window. I ran after you.'

The morgue was half a mile from Hallinan's Mansions. It was attached to a nursing home run by nuns. The dead had been old. They had exhausted their contributory role. Few people came to mourn them. An occasional clump of relatives studied one from a distance.

A nun looked up when the children came in, a dark figure in a corner on a hard chair supplying the creak and rustle of continuous prayer. They kept their heads lowered and joined their hands piously and she let them pass. They walked between the high narrow beds of the dead and looked into their faces. The corpses were not like ordinary old people. They had been laid out in the blue and brown habits of the Legion of Mary or the Order of St Francis to coax them into spiritual company. All the cunning and anger was gone from their faces. They were like shrivelled babies, paper-thin, perplexed. One could tell at a glance that their souls, black or white, had taken flight.

'My da took a strap to me,' Dandy mumbled at the polite remains of an old gentleman.

'What?'

'You heard. He leathered me.' For the first time that day Nan looked straight at her. Dandy had a black eye like a scrapping boy and the side of her jaw was the colour of an orchid.

'Oh, Lord, Dandy, why?'

'I came home late. I was out on a date.'

'You can't let him treat you like that,' she whispered angrily. 'Just because he's your father he can't do what he wants.' She stopped, remembering. Fathers. Dandy was crying. Tears poured over her blackened face, she snuffled over the old man. Nan put out a hand. 'Dandy – my father's awful too. He's done something terrible. He's changed our name.'

'Your name?' Dandy's swimming eyes widened with interest.

'He's done it by deed poll. I'm not Nan Cantwell any more. He's changed our name to Webster.' She found she was crying too. The nun glared at them with sharp suspicion seeing the old man so richly mourned.

'Let's get out of here,' Dandy sniffed and she steered Nan into the bright sunlight.

They went to the park. They pulled hawthorn from the hedges and adorned their hair with sprigs. 'Let's run away,' Nan begged.

Dandy made a face. 'We're too young.'

'Nobody cares about that. We could get jobs in shops or factories. We could stay in boarding houses.' It was like a light inside her, the thought of adventure. Once again her head swam as when she had tasted wine. 'If we ate very little food we could save some money. We could send for Mary and our mothers.'

'We could get fellas to take us out to high tea.'

'Well. Yes.'

Dandy laughed, a careless explosion that creased her damaged face. 'You eejit! You baby! You wouldn't last a day.'

'I'm not a baby!' Nan protested. 'I'm just like you.' She pulled at lumps of grass. 'I've got the curse.' She waited excitedly for her friend to react. Dandy lay down in the grass. She glared at the sky. She rolled over and the little spiky blossoms hopped from her hair.

'You're as green as mouldy cheese,' she said. She watched

Nan sadly through her puffy eyes. 'Do you really think I'd go away?'

'You can't stay.'

'I live in the real world. I always have. There's nowhere else.'

'I'm always looking for the real world. Hardly anything seems real,' Nan said.

'You're a liar, Nan Cantwell. Why do you wrap your bust? You've got a lively figure. You could have your pick.'

'I don't want my pick.' Nan's voice was high and bleak. 'I don't like fellows. You never liked them either.'

'Well, I can tell you they're the only thing. When a fellow puts his arms around you and kisses you, you float away – it's like your first Communion.'

Nan looked at her for a long time. She did not seem happier for all this floating away. The bruises on her face made her older and harder. She seemed restless and defiant. She could not see it but her fellow was just like any other man causing trouble. She reached for Dandy's hand. 'They're not the only thing,' she said. 'There's still me – your best friend.'

Dandy thought about this and she shook her head. 'But you ran after me!' Nan insisted. 'You wanted to see me.' 'I had to *see* you,' Dandy said. 'I needed an excuse to get out of the house. It was all right to be with you. My da likes you.'

'But it helped, didn't it, to talk?'

Dandy shrugged. 'It helped to pass the time. Max won't be here until three.' She frowned. 'It must be nearly that now. I'm meeting Max here. You have to go now.'

Nan scrambled to her feet and ran.

'Na-an!' Dandy's voice was full of penitence. She knew she ought to take no notice but she slowed down and then she looked back and was bewildered to see a little girl with red hair and a yellow dress sprawled in the grass. 'What do you want?' she shouted back. 'Don't go home,' Dandy begged. 'Please don't go home.'

Nan scuffed her boots in the grass. She walked back nonchalantly.

'Oh, go away!' Dandy contradicted in anguish. 'You can't stay here. Just wait for me somewhere. If I come home without you I'll be killed.'

'Get killed,' Nan bawled. 'See if I care.' She raced away as if something was chasing her. The low branches of a tree clawed her face. After a time she was out of breath and she sat down among ferns in a shady place beneath the trees. She was not waiting for Dandy. She was resting because she was tired. Soon she saw the dark and stiff-limbed figure of a boy walk across the green part of the park, his arms swinging like socks on a clothes line. When Dandy saw him she stood up and waited for him and they stalked off into a valley of shrubs and brambles. Nan wanted to cry. She wrapped her arms around her legs and rocked back and forth to help herself but it only made her sleepy and after a few minutes she put her head down and sucked on her knee and dozed. She dreamed that she was in the park and was being watched by an Indian woman who sat on a bench and stared at her. The woman had a small jewel in the side of her nose. She was eating an ice-cream cone. A group of children stood in a half-circle and gaped at her, partly in envy of the ice but more because of the novelty of a mahogany-coloured lady on a park bench, par-celled in gold and purple from head to foot when everyone else was showing off their arms to the sun.

She woke when Dandy shook her shoulders. 'It's me,' she grinned. 'Wakey. Time to go home.' Nan peered at her sleep-ily. Her face seemed softer, more healed, in spite of the ugly marks that were scribbled on her flushed face; she looked soft and pretty now.

Dandy pulled Nan to her feet. 'Thanks, pal. I'll do the same for you sometime.' Nan detached herself coldly. 'I'm not speaking to you,' she said. She walked ahead. When they came to the shops Nan was impeded by a young woman with a pram staring longingly into a sweet shop. Dandy caught up with her. 'I know how it's done,' she hissed. 'I know the facts.' 'The facts?' Nan stared at an arrangement of Clarnico Iced

Caramels. 'Men and women. He told me. It's awful.' The words sat on the back of Nan's neck where they pricked her with ice-cold curiosity. She hurried on. Dandy followed her, all the way to her gate, skittish with her blasted awful secrets. She was trying to shut the gate when Dandy said: 'What did you make of the darkie in the park? Ali Baba and her ice-cream cone?'

'She wasn't Arabian,' Nan murmured coolly. 'She was Indian.' A pulse began to beat in her throat. She frowned at Dandy in alarm. She shook her head. 'There was no one there. It was a dream. You imagined it.'

'Not me. I live in the real world, remember? So long, Sou'Webster!' She laughed and raced back to her own house. She didn't care about anything.

She kept thinking of the faces she had seen in the morgue. She felt that she was one of them, that her soul had been taken away with her name. Resentment confined and pinched her like her party frock that was too small. She cooked a meal for herself without bothering to ask Mary if she was hungry. When she had fed the leftover scraps of rasher and egg to Bertie, she picked him up and brought him, under her arm, to the coal shed. She told herself that she had fetched him for company but in truth she wanted to see if the hen or the cat could be provoked. Mary was in the shed. She squatted on the piles of sacking near the hen. She had something in the lap of her dress that looked like a pine cone. She was smiling and crooning to herself. When Nan pushed in the door she cupped her hands over the thing in her lap and pushed it behind her.

'What have you got there?' Nan said.

'Nothing. Only a hedgehog.'

Nan dropped the cat and it fled into the garden gratefully. 'Mary Webster,' she taunted spitefully. Mary beamed. She picked up the hen and stroked its head. 'Mary *Hilda* Webster,' Nan inserted the hated middle name. Mary made a good-humoured face. Nan glared at her and then stormed back into the house. She went upstairs. There was a light showing under her mother's door but she did not go in. She went to the lavatory. She still had the curse.

She was woken after midnight by father coming in with a truculent banging of doors. Mary was asleep beside her. Her harmless plaits poked out on to the pillow. She felt sorry for having been so mean. She put an arm around her. Mary's sleeping arm instantly embraced her with forgiveness.

There was another disturbance sometime before morning. The silence of the night was slashed by a scream. It was like the night of the cats, only it wasn't cats; it was a woman's voice, terrible, a ragged shriek ending with a gurgle as if her throat had been severed with a knife. Nan awoke sighing with dread. She had been in the middle of a dream. She was in the morgue, walking between the mortuary beds. She stopped to look at the face of a departed one and found that she was gazing into the black open eyes of the Indian woman which were alert and full of spite. She sat trembling until she heard, with relief, the eager clatter of father's bare feet on the stairs. They crept down after him, Mary, Nan and mother, holding each other for bravery. They were disappointed to find that it was only Elizabeth the hen, protesting because Mary's hedgehog had snuggled under her wing for warmth.

The Potato Gatherers

BRIAN FRIEL

November frost had starched the flat countryside into silent rigidity. The 'rat-tat-tat' of the tractor's exhaust drilled into the clean, hard air but did not penetrate it; each staccato sound broke off as if it had been nipped. Hunched over the driver's wheel sat Kelly, the owner, a rock of a man with a huge head and broken fingernails, and in the trailer behind were his four potato gatherers – two young men, permanent farm hands, and the two boys he had hired for the day. At six o'clock in the morning, they were the only living things in that part of County Tyrone.

The boys chatted incessantly. They stood at the front of the trailer, legs apart, hands in their pockets, their faces pressed forward into the icy rush of air, their senses edged for perception. Joe, the elder of the two – he was thirteen and had worked for Kelly on two previous occasions – might have been quieter, but his brother's excitement was infectious. For this was Philly's first job, his first time to take a day off from school to earn money, his first opportunity to prove that he was a man at twelve years of age. His energy was a burden to him. Behind them, on the floor of the trailer, the two farm hands lay sprawled in half sleep.

Twice the boys had to cheer. The first was when they were passing Dicey O'Donnell's house, and Philly, who was in the same class as Dicey, called across to the thatched, smokeless building, 'Remember me to all the boys, Dicey!' The second time was when they came to the school itself. It was then that Kelly turned to them and growled to them to shut up.

'Do you want the whole country to know you're taking the day off?' he said. 'Save your breath for your work.'

When Kelly faced back to the road ahead, Philly stuck his thumbs in his ears, put out his tongue, and wriggled his fingers at the back of Kelly's head. Then, suddenly forgetting him, he said, 'Tell me, Joe, what are you going to buy?'

'Buy?'

'With the money we get today. I know what I'm getting – a shotgun. Bang! Bang! Bang! Right there, mistah. Jist you put your two hands up above your head and I reckon you'll live a little longer.' He menaced Kelly's neck.

'Agh!' said Joe derisively.

'True as God, Joe. I can get it for seven shillings – an old one that's lying in Tom Tracy's father's barn. Tom told me he would sell it for seven shillings.'

'Who would sell it?'

'Tom.'

'Steal it, you mean. From his old fella.'

'His old fella has a new one. This one's not wanted.' He sighted along an imaginary barrel and picked out an unsuspecting sparrow in the hedge. 'Bang! Never knew what hit you, did you? What are you going to buy, Joe?'

'I don't know. There won't be much to buy with. Maybe – naw, I don't know. Depends on what Ma gaves us back.'

'A bicycle, Joe. What about a bike? Quinn would give his away for a packet of cigarettes. You up on the saddle, Joe, and me on the crossbar. Out to the millrace every evening. Me shooting all the rabbits along the way. Bang! Bang! Bang! What about a bike, Joe?'

'I don't know. I don't know.'

'What did she give you back the last time?'

'I can't remember.'

'Ten shillings? More? What did you buy then? A leather belt? A set of rabbit snares?'

'I don't think I got anything back. Maybe a shilling. I don't remember.'

'A shilling! One lousy shilling out of fourteen! Do you know what I'm going to buy?' He hunched his shoulders and lowered his head between them. One eye closed in a huge wink. 'Tell no one? Promise?'

'What?'

'A gaff. See?'

'What about the gun?'

'It can wait until next year. But a gaff, Joe. See? Old Philly down there beside the Black Pool. A big salmon. A beaut. Flat on my belly, and – *phwist!* – there he is on the bank, the gaff stuck in his guts.' He clasped his middle and writhed in agony, imitating the fish. Then his act switched suddenly back to cowboys and he drew from both holsters at a cat sneaking home along the hedge. 'Bang! Bang! That sure settled you, boy. Where *is* this potato territory, mistah? Ah want to show you hombres what work is. What's a-keeping this old tractor-buggy?'

'We're jist about there, Mistah Philly, sir,' said Joe. 'Ah reckon you'll show us, OK. You'll show us.'

The field was a two-acre rectangle bordered by a low hedge. The ridges of potatoes stretched lengthwise in straight, black lines. Kelly unfastened the trailer and hooked up the mechanical digger. The two labourers stood with their hands in their pockets and scowled around them, cigarettes hanging from their lips.

'You two take the far side,' Kelly told them. 'And Joe, you

and –' He could not remember the name. 'You and the lad there, you two take this side. You show him what to do, Joe.' He climbed up on the tractor seat. 'And remember,' he called over his shoulder, 'if the school-attendance officer appears, it's up to you to run. I never seen you. I never heard of you.'

The tractor moved forward into the first ridges, throwing up a spray of brown earth behind it as it went.

'Right,' said Joe. 'What we do is this, Philly. When the digger passes, we gather the spuds into these buckets and then carry the buckets to the sacks and fill them. Then back again to fill the buckets. And back to the sacks. OK, mistah?'

'OK, mistah. Child's play. What does he want four of us for? I could do the whole field myself – one hand tied behind my back.'

Joe smiled at him. 'Come on, then. Let's see you.'

'Just you watch,' said Philly. He grabbed a bucket and ran stumbling across the broken ground. His small frame bent over the clay and his thin arms worked madly. Before Joe had begun gathering, Philly's voice called to him. 'Joe! Look! Full already! Not bad, eh?'

'Take your time,' Joe called back.

'And look, Joe! Look!' Philly held his hands out for his brother's inspection. They were coated with earth.

'How's that, Joe? They'll soon be as hard as Kelly's!'

Joe laughed. 'Take it easy, Philly. No rush.'

But Philly was already stooped again over his work, and when Joe was emptying his first bucket into the sack, Philly was emptying his third. He gave Joe the huge wink again and raced off.

Kelly turned at the bottom of the field and came back up. Philly was standing waiting for him.

'What you need is a double digger, Mr Kelly!' he called as the tractor passed. But Kelly's eyes never left the ridges in front of him. A flock of seagulls swooped and dipped behind the tractor, fluttering down to catch worms in the newly turned earth. The boy raced off with his bucket.

'How's it going?' shouted Joe after another twenty minutes. Philly was too busy to answer.

A pale sun appeared about eight-thirty. It was not strong enough to soften the earth, but it loosened sounds – cars along the road, birds in the naked trees, cattle let out for the day. The clay became damp under it but did not thaw. The tractor exulted in its new freedom and its spluttering filled the countryside.

'I've been thinking,' said Philly when he met Joe at a sack. 'Do you know what I'm going to get, Joe? A scout knife with one of those leather scabbards. Four shillings in Byrne's shop. Great for skinning a rabbit.' He held his hands out from his sides now, because they were raw in places. 'Yeah. A scout knife with a leather scabbard.'

'A scout knife,' Joe repeated.

'You always have to carry a scout knife in case your gun won't fire or your powder gets wet. And when you're swimming underwater, you can always carry a knife between your teeth.'

'We'll have near twenty ridges done before noon,' said Joe.

'He should have a double digger. I told him that. Too slow, mistah. Too doggone slow. Tell me, Joe, have you made up your mind yet?'

'What about?'

'What you're going to buy, stupid.'

'Aw, naw. Naw . . . I don't know yet.'

Philly turned to his work again and was about to begin, when the school bell rang. He dropped his bucket and danced back to his brother. 'Listen! Joe! Listen!' He caught fistfuls of his hair and tugged his head from side to side. 'Listen! Listen! Ha, ha ha! Ho, ho, ho! Come on, you fat, silly, silly scholars and get to your lessons! Come on, come on, come on, come on. No dallying! Speed it up! Get a move on! Hurry! Hurry! Hurry! "And where are the O'Boyle brothers today? Eh? Where are they? Gathering potatoes? What's that I hear? What? What?"'

'Look out, lad!' roared Kelly.

The tractor passed within inches of Philly's legs. He jumped out of its way in time, but a fountain of clay fell on his head and shoulders. Joe ran to his side.

'Are you all right, Philly? Are you O K?'

'Tried to get me, that's what he did, the dirty cattle thief. Tried to get me.'

'You O K, mistah? Reckon you'll live?'

'Sure, mistah. Take more'n that ole coyote to scare me. Come on, mistah. We'll show him what men we really are.' He shook his jacket and hair and hitched up his trousers. 'Would you swap now, Joe?'

'Swap what?'

'Swap places with those poor eejits back there?' He jerked his thumb in the direction of the school.

'No sir,' said Joe. 'Not me.'

'Nor me neither, mistah. Meet you in the saloon.' He swaggered off, holding his hands as if they were delicate things, not part of him.

They broke off for lunch at noon. By then, the sun was high and brave but still of little use. With the engine of the tractor cut off, for a brief time there was a self-conscious silence, which became relaxed and natural when the sparrows, now audible, began to chirp. The seagulls squabbled over the latest turned earth and a cautious puff of wind stirred the branches of the tall trees. Kelly adjusted the digger while he ate. On the far side of the field, the two labourers stretched themselves on sacks and conversed in monosyllables. Joe and Philly sat on upturned buckets. For lunch they each had half a scone of home-made soda bread, cut into thick slices and skimmed with butter. They washed it down with mouthfuls of cold tea from a bottle. After they had eaten, Joe threw the crusts to the gulls, gathered up the newspapers in which the bread had been wrapped, emptied out the remains of the tea, and put the bottle and the papers into his jacket pocket. Then he stood up and stretched himself.

'My back's getting stiff,' he said.

Philly sat with his elbows on his knees and studied the palms of his hands.

'Sore?' asked Joe.

'What?'

'Your hands. Are they hurting you?'

'They're OK,' said Philly. 'Tough as leather. But the clay's sore. Gets right into every cut and away up your nails.' He held his arms out. 'They're shaking,' he said. 'Look.'

'That's the way they go,' said Joe. 'But they'll – Listen! Do you hear?'

'Hear what?'

'Lunchtime at school. They must be playing football in the playground.'

The sounds of high, delighted squealing came intermittently when the wind sighed. They listened to it with their heads uplifted, their faces broadening with memory.

'We'll get a hammering tomorrow,' said Joe. 'Six on each hand.'

'It's going to be a scout knife,' Philly said. 'I've decided on that.'

'She mightn't give us anything back. Depends on how much she needs herself.'

'She said she would. She promised. Have you decided yet?'

'I'm still thinking,' said Joe.

The tractor roared suddenly, scattering every other sound.

'Come on, mistah,' said the older one. 'Four more hours to go. Saddle up your horse.'

'Coming. Coming,' Philly replied. His voice was sharp with irritation.

The sun was a failure. It held its position in the sky and flooded the countryside with light but could not warm it. Even before it had begun to slip to the west, the damp ground had become glossy again, and before the afternoon was spent, patches of white frost were appearing on higher ground. Now the boys were working automatically, their minds acquiescing in what their bodies did. They no longer straightened up; the world was their feet and the hard clay and the potatoes and their hands and the buckets and the sacks. Their ears told them where the tractor was, at the bottom of the field, turning, approaching. Their muscles had become adjusted to their stooped position, and as long as the boys kept within the established pattern of movement their arms and hands and legs and shoulders seemed to float as if they were free of gravity. But if something new was expected from the limbs – a piece of glass to be thrown in to the hedge, a quick stepping back to avoid the digger – then their bodies shuddered with pain and the tall trees reeled and the hedges rose to the sky.

Dicey O'Donnell gave them a shout from the road on his way home from school. 'Hi! Joe! Philly!'

They did not hear him. He waited until the tractor turned. 'Hi! Hi! Philly! Joe! Youse are for it the morrow. I'm telling youse. He knows where youse are. He says he's going to beat the scruff out of youse the morrow. Youse are in for it, all right. Blue murder! Bloody hell! True as God!'

'Will I put a bullet in him, mistah?' said Joe to Philly.

Philly did not answer. He thought he was going to fall, and his greatest fear was that he might fall in front of the tractor, because now the tractor's exhaust had only one sound, fixed for ever in his head, and unless he saw the machine he could not tell whether it was near him or far away. The 'rat-tat-tat' was a finger tapping in his head, drumming at the back of his eyes.

'Vamoose, O'Donnell!' called Joe. 'You annoy us. Vamoose.'

O'Donnell said something more about the reception they could expect the next day, but he got tired of calling to two stooped backs and he went off home.

The last pair of ridges was turned when the sky had veiled itself for dusk. The two brothers and the two labourers worked on until they met in the middle. Now the field was all brown, all flat, except for the filled sacks that patterned it. Kelly was satisfied; his lips formed an O and he blew through them as if he were trying to whistle. He detached the digger and hooked up the trailer. 'All aboard!' he shouted, in an effort at levity.

On the way home, the labourers seemed to be fully awake, for the first time since morning. They stood in the trailer where the boys had stood at dawn, behind Kelly's head and facing the road before them. They chatted and guffawed and made plans for a dance that night. When they met people they knew along the way, they saluted extravagantly. At the crossroads, they began to wrestle, and Kelly had to tell them to watch out or they would fall over the side. But he did not sound angry.

Joe sat on the floor, his legs straight out before him, his back resting against the side of the trailer. Philly lay flat out, his head cushioned on his brother's lap. Above him, the sky spread out, grey, motionless, enigmatic. The warmth from Joe's body made him drowsy. He wished the journey home to go on for ever, the sound of the tractor engine to anaesthetize his mind for ever. He knew that if the movement and the sound were to cease, the pain of his body would be unbearable.

'We're nearly there,' said Joe quietly. 'Are you asleep?' Philly did not answer. 'Mistah! Are you asleep, mistah?'

'No.'

Darkness came quickly, and when the last trace of light disappeared the countryside became taut with frost. The head-lamps of the tractor glowed yellow in the cold air.

'Philly! Are you awake, mistah?'

'What?'

'I've been thinking,' said Joe slowly. 'And do you know what I think? I think I've made up my mind now.'

One of the labourers burst into song.

'"If I were a blackbird, I'd whistle and sing, and I'd follow the ship that my true love sails in."'

His mate joined him at the second line and their voices exploded in the stiff night.

'Do you know what I'm going to buy?' Joe said, speaking

more loudly. 'If she gives us something back, that is. Mistah! Mistah Philly! Are you listening? I'm going to buy a pair of red silk socks.'

He waited for approval from Philly. When none came, he shook his brother's head. 'Do you hear, mistah? Red silk socks – the kind Jojo Teague wears. What about that, eh? What do you think?'

Philly stirred and half raised his head from his brother's lap. 'I think you're daft,' he said in an exhausted, sullen voice. 'Ma won't give us back enough to buy anything much. No more than a shilling. You knew it all the time.' He lay down again and in a moment he was fast asleep.

Joe held his brother's head against the motion of the trailer and repeated the words 'red silk socks' to himself again and again, nodding each time at the wisdom of his decision.

Glossary

Aughrim was lost (136)	battle was lost (from the Battle of Aughrim, 1691)
avic (55)	a mhic (Irish term of affection)
capernoity (133)	muddle-headedness
caubeen (57)	hat
codding (23)	teasing
crack (47)	conversation
dinging (137)	dark-coloured
fitch (25)	polecat
flits (16)	removals
gaff (152)	hook (used for landing large fish)
garda (55)	policeman
gossoon (58)	child
Grangegorman (138)	Dublin mental hospital
handselled (138)	gave a present
IHS (134)	abbreviation for Jesus, from Greek
mind (15,70)	remember
on the pig's back (16)	in clover
praties (59)	potatoes
quare (16, 22)	queer
redd up (16)	tidy, clean up
scoil (133)	school (Irish)
sheeps' lights (135)	offal
sheugh (21)	ditch
thon (70, 73)	that
weans (27)	children
Well, how are you, Burke! (14)	Well, what do you make of that!
wheen (27)	a few, good many

Acknowledgements

The editors and publishers gratefully acknowledge permission to reproduce the following copyright material in this book:

'The Confirmation Suit' by Brendan Behan, reprinted by permisson of Beatrice Behan; 'Holy Pictures' by Clare Boylan, from *Holy Pictures*, reprinted by permisson of Hamish Hamilton; 'The Potato Gatherers' by Brian Friel, reprinted by permission of Gallery Press; 'Arcady' by E. L. Kennedy, from *Twelve in Arcady*, reprinted by permission of Blackstaff Press Ltd; 'My Vocation' by Mary Lavin, from *The Stories of Mary Lavin* (Constable and Co. Ltd), reprinted by permisson of A. D. Peters; 'Sammy Gorman and the Light' by Joan Lingard, reprinted by permission of David Higham Associates Ltd; 'Last Bus for Christmas' by Patricia Lynch, from *Strangers at the Fair* (Richview Press); 'The Lion' by Walter Macken, from *God Made Sunday and other stories*, reprinted by permission of Macmillan; 'The Exercise' by Bernard MacLaverty, from *Secrets*, reprinted by permission of Blackstaff Press Ltd; 'The Decision' by Stella Mahon, from *Sisters*, reprinted by permission of Blackstaff Press Ltd; 'Gypsy' by Sam McBratney, reprinted by permission of the author; 'Traffic Jam' by Frank Murphy, from *Links 1*, reprinted by permission of the Educational Company of Ireland (a trading unit of Smurfit Ireland Ltd); 'The Rug' by Edna O'Brien, from *The Love Object* (Jonathan Cape Ltd), reprinted by permission of A. M. Heath; 'The Genius' by Frank O'Connor, from *The Stories of Frank O'Connor* (Hamish Hamilton), reprinted by permission of A. D. Peters and Co. Ltd; 'The Trout' by Sean O'Faolain, from *The Man Who Invented Sin* (1948), reprinted by permission of Devin-Adair Company (USA); 'Three Lambs' by Liam O'Flaherty, from *The Short Stories of Liam O'Flaherty*, reprinted by permission of Jonathan Cape Ltd; 'Sunflowers in the Snow' by

Some other books you might enjoy

THE WILD RIDE AND OTHER SCOTTISH STORIES

ed. Gordon Jarvie

A spirited anthology of modern short stories from Scotland, ranging widely through ghost stories, adventure, drama and humour.

GUARDIAN ANGELS

ed. Stephanie Nettell

An anthology of stories specially written to commemorate the prestigious *Guardian* Children's Book Award's twentieth anniversary.

TALES FOR THE TELLING

Edna O'Brien

A collection of heroic Irish tales to stir the imagination.

THE GNOME FACTORY AND OTHER STORIES

James Reeves

The imagination of James Reeves's stories and the wit of Edward Ardizzone's drawings combine to make this enchanting collection.

CHOCOLATE PORRIDGE AND OTHER STORIES

Margaret Mahy

Here is a collection of twenty-one stories, full of fun and surprises, that will captivate every reader.

DON'T COUNT YOUR CHICKENS AND OTHER FABULOUS FABLES

Mark Cohen

Always fun, and often funny, this is a wide-ranging collection of fables from all around the world, for both children and adults to enjoy.

NEVER MEDDLE WITH MAGIC AND OTHER STORIES

Chosen by Barbara Ireson

Fifty fabulous stories full of magic and mischief, fun and fantasy. Stories short and long, funny stories, sad stories, 'once upon a time' stories, fairy tales and ghost stories, birthday stories and Christmas stories – there's something for everyone in this enticing collection.

MR CORBETT'S GHOST
AND OTHER STORIES

Three chilling stories for those who like a shivery thrill.

SWEETS FROM A STRANGER
AND OTHER STRANGE TALES
Nicholas Fisk

A collection of imaginative and macabre science fiction stories.

MESSAGES
Marjorie Darke

A collection of shivery tales which you'd better not read alone . . .

IMAGINE THAT!
Sara and Stephen Corrin

Fifteen fantastic tales, mostly traditional, from all over the world, including China and Asia.

THE RUNAWAY SHOES
AND OTHER STORIES

Chosen by Barbara Ireson

With such well-known writers included as E. Nesbit and Arthur Ransome along with names less familiar, this is a wide-ranging anthology providing a wealth of delightful stories to be read again and again.

A THIEF IN THE VILLAGE
AND OTHER STORIES

James Berry

Wonderfully atmospheric, rich and moving, these very contemporary narratives bring alive the setting and culture highly relevant to today's multi-ethnic Britain.

THE GHOST'S COMPANION

ed. Peter Haining

Thrilling ghost stories by well-known writers – and the incidents which first gave them the idea.